VIOLET DAINTY

SNAPSHOTS OF

LIFE

10 MINUTE TALES FROM EVERYDAY FOLK

 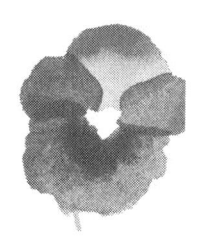

Violet Dainty represents a group of authors named in the back part of the book - "Meet the Writers" who collectively own the copyright of this book.

It is a work of fiction. Names, characters, places, and incidents either are the product of the author's imagination or are used fictitiously. Any resemblance to actual persons, living or dead, events, or location is entirely coincidental.

All rights reserved. No part of this book may be reproduced in any form on by an electronic or mechanical means, including information storage and retrieval systems, without permission in writing from one of the writers (Named in the part "Meet the Writers") and only relating to her part/story in the book

Any royalties from this publication will be used for the benefit of the "Away with Words" group members in their writing journey.

ISBN: 9798859038497 (paperback)

Printed by Amazon

First Edition: October 2023

Contents

Preface	5
Day in the Life of a Postie	7
George of The Grange	21
Be Careful What You Wish For	39
The Last Goodbye	47
The Surprise	53
Rescued	63
The Old Tin Box	71
Coming Home	81
The Dance	87
Frederick Peverill	101

Festival Child	113
The Prom	127
Belle	145
Spreading my Wings @ The Comfy Nest	163
Diggle Junction	171
The Yellow Raincoat	185
The Secret	197
End of Term Final Feast	211
Meet The Writers	221

Preface

The pen name Violet Dainty represents an eclectic group of women who come together weekly under the collective name "A Way with Words." They have a common bond, each having a love of the written word in its many forms.

Writing can function as therapy, the women provide support, motivation, and inspiration to each other. It enables, empowers, and promotes a sense of achievement within the group. It can be a cathartic experience.

This book has come together in a joint venture of short story writing and sharing within the group. The loyalties from this book will go to resources for the group to further their writing journey.

You can read about the writers and which stories they contributed in the About the Writers section at the back of the book.

We hope you really enjoy our coffee table read; our stories come from the heart ... sit back and enjoy!

A day in the life of a postie

Liam was first down, as usual, having had a shower and a quick shave, before getting dressed in his red polo shirt, black shorts, and baseball cap. Glancing in the mirror, he proudly tapped the logo on his left chest.

He could hear his mum stirring next door and, before long, she appeared on the landing, wearing her full length, mint green, velvety dressing gown and her dark red furry slippers. She yawned luxuriously as she pulled her fingers through her dyed, darkish blond hair, then pushed her glasses back into place with her other hand. There were a few lines in that face – experience rather than sadness – and it was soft and plump, full of love and hopeful expectation.

"Oh Ma! You don't have to get up!"

"Well, you'll be out most of the day, son! You know I like to have a cup of tea with you before you go out, even if I do go back to bed sometimes! You're doing well with these early starts."

"I've settled into it ok; I reckon. After all, I've never been one for staying out late, clubbing and such, you know that."

"Yeah, you're a good boy, Liam."

Drawing himself up to his full height, he retorted, sharply,

"You'd better stop calling me a 'good boy' Ma! It's not dignified, at my stage in life!"

"Hark at you!" she mocked, laughing at the same time. "I'll fill the kettle and make you a bacon sandwich to put you on. You made a cheese sandwich for your dinner already, didn't you. . ."

He followed her downstairs, got the mugs out and the teabags, and made the tea while she got their breakfast going.

"I fancied a bacon sandwich myself once I suggested it. Ketchup or brown sauce?"

They were soon eating, slurping the tea. He ate in a hurry, watching the clock and pacing himself against it. She took small bites and sipped her tea delicately, in no rush.

He was the only one still at home. Having lost her husband, Mick, way too young, she felt all the more responsible for parenting their children, taking every care to try to do a good job.

Looking at him now, with his neat haircut, short at the sides and longer on top, his smooth face, with only a few acne scars to blemish it, his kind, blue eyes, and his smart postal uniform, she felt he was turning out very well. Thank the Lord, his older brother and sister seemed to be well settled in decent jobs too. If you can earn a living, and pay your bills, have a little bit spare for some entertainment and occasional holiday – well, life's not so bad.

She felt more settled now too. Remaining single was more just how it turned out than a life choice, but her family all stayed connected. Probably far more so than if her Mick had still been alive. She knew that they felt protective towards her, and wanted to shelter her…

"I'm gonna do it, Ma."

"What was that Liam? I'm sorry, son, I was miles away!"

"I'm going to ask her."

"Ask her what? Oh!"

"Yeah, that's right. I'm going to ask her to marry me!"

"Oh, Liam! That's . . . Wow!"

"You're not worried it's too soon?"

"Well, only if you are, son. Let me see, you've been going steady now for…"

"She's the one for me, Ma! I'm certain of it. And I'm sure she feels the same way."

"Liam, that's wonderful news. I've always felt happy with her, from the first day you brought her home for her tea. When are you going to ask her?"

"I was thinking, Ma, if it's all right with you, when you go away this weekend, could I use the kitchen? I'd like to try to cook her a special tea. You've been teaching me how to do proper roast dinners with nice veggies and stuffing and gravy. I thought I'd do a very simple starter – maybe some chilled mackerel pâte with toast, because I could do that in advance. And maybe a cheesecake with a raspberry or blueberry compote because I could do that the day before and chill it in the fridge. I'll save some for you of course!"

"Oh, yes. She'll know you've gone to some trouble when you serve her a three-course tea! I think she'll be very pleased. Yes, of course you have my permission to use our kitchen. Not just my kitchen, son! Your roasts are coming on a treat! You've more than earned the right to use the oven!"

"Ah flip, Ma, I gotta go!"

"Drive carefully, son"

"Always!"

She watched him through the open front door as he jumped into the car and headed off to the depot. "So, he really is grown up, now," she thought to herself, wistfully, but also with pride.

He'd made it in time, he didn't like feeling in a rush, which is why he usually set off that bit earlier and took time to glance at a paper while he had his coffee in the staff lounge. This morning, he'd had to put a drop of cold water in the coffee so that he could down it that bit faster but, no worries.

First there was a bit of sorting to do. The machine read the postcodes successfully on most of the letters but there were always a few which failed the automatic reader – due to wobbly handwriting or stamps obscuring part of the postcode. After that, he got has black canvas bag filled up with the post destined for the streets he had become so familiar with. He also had several parcels to deliver. He stowed them all into the red postal van assigned for his use and set off for his area.

Once he had parked up, he knew that there were a few hours of walking ahead of him. He didn't mind that. The bag was quite heavy at first, but it got lighter as he delivered more and more of the letters. Occasionally, he had to return to the van and drive it to a different location within his area, and he picked up the parcels from the van once he was near to their destination.

Everything was routine, that day, as on all the other days since he had started the job. He had been doing it for a few years now, saving up all

he could, as he had known for some time that Rachel was special too him. In recent months, he had become more and more certain that he wanted to marry her. Now, he really felt that the timing was right. He loved everything about her.

Sure, she was quite a bit older than him.

At first, that made him think that there was no way they would have any future together – but they just got on so well that, before many weeks had passed, the age gap no longer seemed relevant.

They had the strangest things in common: online games that they both already played and which they now played together most evenings. They both liked Sci-Fi films and detective dramas. Even liking quite a few of the same bands – and then finding they also liked the bands that they introduced to each other, by sharing you-tube links. They both disliked swimming. She did some running, which he hated, but he liked orienteering and he introduced her to the sport – which she instantly took a liking to as being so much more interesting than just running – she loved the coloured maps and all the colour-coded features within them – and really liked that it was a point-to-point activity with the chance to pick your own route, instead of just going round a track!

He had arrived at the house where the big parcel was to be delivered: "Number 84 – that's it". It was a bulky and fairly heavy parcel, so he had to lean it against the wall while he rang the doorbell. The door was answered by a young man with long, dark brown hair, a wispy kind of beard and brown eyes.

"Oh, great!" he said. "Do I have to sign for it?"

"Who is it? Oh! Shit!"

Liam froze. The woman who had walked up behind the man was Rachel, *his* Rachel or, that's what he'd thought!

What was she doing here with this young fellow – oh my God – he seemed barely out of school!

He suddenly unfroze himself, pushed the parcel into the young man's arms, turned tail and walked away, and his walk almost broke into a run – he wanted to run – but he just kept enough control of himself to keep to a really tense walk – and he wanted to cry – but he shook his head to shake the tears back so they wouldn't spill down his stiffly grimacing face.

"Liam! Liam! Come back! Let me explain!"

Rachel was calling down the street at him as he raced away. No way was he going back! His Rachel was there in that man's house, early in the morning, and he was really young even a lot younger than Liam himself. Maybe that's her thing, he thought, bitterly, and yet, she was so loving to him, and had declared her love to him. How can she be there with someone else, so comfortable with someone else? Had he misjudged her? had he misjudged everything. Could he trust anything that he had thought to be certain, and true?

Thank Christ, he only had those last couple of parcels to deliver on the other side of the village, then he could return to base, deposit the keys, and get off home, his shift over for the day. Liam hadn't looked back but he knew that Rachel hadn't caught up with him. Maybe she had some explaining to do to that man, just as she would to him. He drove around to a quiet lane surrounded by trees on both sides and parked up where the lane had a passing place. Now, the tears fell, and he let them. His polo shirt became damp against his chest.

Had he really got her so wrong? Was she a two-timing cougar who had just been stringing him along? Taken advantage of his relative youth and naivety? Why would she? He had precious little money and, anyway, he had not even told her how much of a very small amount he had gradually saved up. Neither of them had expensive tastes. She really seemed to enjoy spending time with him, online and in real life. Sharing a portion of fish and chips over a movie was their idea of bliss – like when she brought over "Squid Game," or that comedy detective series "Cloth." He smiled at the memory. Then frowned again. His forehead hurt.

Maybe he'd over-reacted. Maybe there was an explanation that didn't involve the horrible thoughts he'd been having. "Oh, please, let there be!" he moaned, gently.

Hearing his own words in the near silence of the parked van, nothing outside but a few birds cawing in the trees, gave him a jolt. He used his fingers to wipe the wetness off his cheeks, wiped them in turn on the sides of his polo shirt, sniffed loudly, and started the van. Just those two parcels, and he could go home.

Thank God there were no great surprises at those properties. Business as usual – apart from the headache which had taken over his skull, and the dull ache of sadness in his chest.

He saw his Ma as he approached home. She was looking out of the window of the front room, as if she had been waiting for him. Unusual. Then she was at the front door to let him in. Very unusual.

"What have you done, Liam?" she whispered. "Rachel's here, and she seems upset."

He frowned deeply, and physically took a step back in surprise.

"What have … I done?" he muttered.

"Just come in and talk to her. I've got a freshly made pot of tea in the kitchen – she's not been here long. I'll pour three cups."

Liam walked into the front room. Rachel was sitting, in one corner of the sofa, but very near the front of it, knees together and twisted to one side, back straight vertical and hands tightly gripped together. Her long brown hair was drawn back off her face with a couple of tortoiseshell patterned slides, and he again noticed the occasional strands of grey, and the few lines on her face – only a few, but certainly more than the young women of his own age would show. She was wearing a flowery patterned dress and a dark red cardigan – the same outfit as she had been wearing earlier when –

"Liam, you rushed off so fast! I wanted to explain but I couldn't come after you as I didn't have any shoes on!"

A detail he hadn't noticed. Was it a bad thing?

She babbled on, before her voice faded,

"Gravel really hurts in bare ... feet..."

"I don't know what you were doing there Rachel," his voice small and flat.

Rachel spoke, more urgently,

"I know, I know! I'm trying to explain – but – it's difficult for me!"

"Difficult for you?", Liam replied sharply Ma was back in the room. "Liam, Liam, give the girl a chance! Can't you see she's upset?

"Look, I've brought the tea" Let's all sit down and drink some."

A few minutes later, Rachel spoke again.

"Yes, Liam, it is. It is difficult for me, and I feel awful for not having told you before, but it's very difficult, and I didn't want to land it on you, when it's not your responsibility and maybe you would never need to know, and maybe you wouldn't want to keep seeing me . . . so I've been scared to tell you . . ."

She was clearly on the verge of tears by the time she finished this little speech. Liam's Ma reached out her arm to touch Rachel's forearm, gave it a gentle squeeze and a little shake to and fro, then returned her hand to the side of her mug of tea. Like everyone else, she had hardly drunk from it, but the fragrance and heat of the tea felt comforting all the same.

Liam's eyes were wide, staring randomly around the room, as he had no idea what Rachel was talking about. But he listened, carefully, as Rachel gave her explanation, haltingly.

"I just don't want to lose you, Liam."

"That was Billy you saw.

"He's 18 years old.

"He was living with his grandparents before, but they've moved into a retirement village – and he's moved to be closer to me.

"He's, my son."

"Your son." Liam repeated the information in a quiet, low voice. He still felt bewildered but was now just beginning to process what Rachel was saying.

"Yes," she almost gasped over the word.

Liam looked over to his Ma. She had remained very quiet and still, to allow Rachel to take her time to speak, and she still showed no signs of reacting. Did she already know? Or was this complete news to her as well. Actually, she was always slow to react to things, as if she felt it was best to process information carefully rather than jump to conclusions. It was one of the wonderful things about her – her calmness in a storm.

Liam had jumped to conclusions.

He had doubted Rachel. How could he have done that? How could he ever have imagined that she might be two-timing him. He might have to keep that from her. Or, he just might have to confess it to her. He'd have to think carefully about that one.

The point is, the news is – the fact is that Rachel has at some stage – well, just over 18 years ago – had a baby. Who was the dad? What was – that – backstory?

It didn't matter. She could now tell him everything. He wished she had felt able to tell him long before . . . but she must have been very young – maybe early teens – that can't have been easy. It's probably something she's always had to treat as a secret from a lot of people. There had been a very long silence in the room as Liam had thought his thoughts and guessed his guesses. Finally, he spoke.

"Rachel, love. Thank you for telling us. I'm sorry I ran off before. I didn't know what to think so I legged it. It's just a bit of a shock. I guess we don't know each other quite as well as I had imagined…"

"I'm so sorry Liam – "

"It's ok – I didn't mean to upset you more! That came out all wrong! I just mean, we've got some fresh things to talk about – to learn about each other. There's plenty of time.

How about . . . would you and Billy like to come round here on Saturday night for your tea?

That is, if he's not already got plans.

We could do it Friday night if he prefers. I'd like to meet him."

George of The Grange

I may as well be on the moon, thought George, as he sat in the lounge of the Grange feeling more than a bit depressed. All the top windowpanes  were bright colourful flower pictures, the red rose of Lancashire, the white rose of Yorkshire and a family coat of arms. It was a warm summer's day, rainbows of refracted light streamed in through the leaded glass illuminating the dull décor. He could see Roses proudly holding their regal heads high, poking up between beautiful bluebells and heathers.

The Grange was a large Victorian house, it was a nice place, he was looked after well, fed, watered, slept in a comfy bed, warm and cosy. It was just like being a plant given all the nutrients it needs, but somehow George thought he'd had finished flowering long ago. It was George's wake up call, he'd been a bit of a loner throughout his life, a confirmed bachelor, didn't have a big friendship group, added to which, many of his friends were "falling off the perch" these days. All doom and gloom …

Between physio sessions, George people watched all day from his beige leather chair at one end of the lounge in front of the television. The same programmes went round and round at the same times every day. Same chair, different day, all running into one long boring lonely existence. He read all the same signs and pictures over and over like a large waiting room Most of the signs were years old anyway, outdated advertisements for healthy eating sitting incongruously alongside new posters inviting "Pure Cremation" Lol …

There was an old dark-mahogany bookcase, with rows of books like retired soldiers standing to attention for show, no-one ever perused the titles. It was a redundant piece of furniture, taking up space till it went to the tip. He smiled to himself as he imagined that, even the furniture was waiting for God! Everyone and everything in here must be waiting to meet the Almighty. He had gone through a recent phase in hospital where he wondered when, and prayed that soon, he would reach the front of the queue, and could toddle off this mortal coil finally. He had always believed that God had a queue of people waiting to enter eternity, everyone had a place in the queue, only thing was no-one knew whether they were at the front or many years back.

How have I come to this? How did I end up in a nursing home?

He was approaching the epilogue of his life, but before his illness, George had been planning the concluding chapter which was still be waiting to be written.

A small, frail looking lady occupied the other beige armchair with a footstool to support her legs. Every day, her white hair was dragged back into a ponytail, she wore a fluffy bright pink dressing gown and striped knitted socks which were all different shades of pink, head bent forward as though she was sleeping.

Occasionally she would call over to George …

"Psssst, over here … are you going out today, can I walk out with you?"

George would nod to pacify her, he thought she was a bit "do lally tap." In his mind, although he didn't even know her name, he had called her moaning Maureen, he tried not to get eye contact with her. It was a very lonely existence even with people around. He was sat all day with only his own thoughts for company going round and round in his head.

He had even entertained the idea of getting his glad rags on and treating Moaning Maureen to a trip to the local pub … just for the hell of it. He could order a taxi, the side doors to the ramp were open, no-one would notice, mind you, he supposed they would if Maureen turned up for her half of cider in her fluffy pink dressing gown Lol.

The highlight of the day was observing and listening to the staff as they moved around doing their work. It made him smile as they talked about swiping left and right on their "App," Ffs ...

"What is swiping left and right? George asked his favourite Helen ...

"Plenty of Fish, it's where most young people look for a date these days George" she quipped.

"Ah that's what we used to say Helen, plenty more fish in the sea, when we got dumped, but we didn't have what you call an App, some people had phones in their house, but they were in mainly in red boxes at the end of the road, it was the lonely-hearts column in the paper, we used to put and Ad in, something like this"

"Single male seeks double-jointed supermodel who owns a brewery and grows her own pot. Access to concert tickets and an open-minded twin sister would be welcomed. Phone 01942 ..."

"OMG George, what ya like!"

George was a bit of a technological dinosaur, he could just about switch on his old computer at home and hadn't done that for some time.

"We have a lady who comes in who is a whizz on computers, she teaches "Silver Surfing" for beginners laughed Helen, should I put you down for it?

"Sounds like a plan, let's do it!" George's sense of humour had him imagining himself in his speedos carrying his surfboard down the beach. He had oceans of memories of long days lying on the naturist beach in his favourite resort in times when very few people went abroad. He had been a "trailblazer", it always brought a smile when he recalled the first time, he told his mum & dad he was going to Australia for the princely sum of £10 as part of the assisted migration scheme offered by the Aussie government.

You going out of your mind? folk like us don't go to them places George" his dad retorted throwing a bemusing look at Clara, his mum. George just laughed, "life is for living" and, shortly after, George became a £10 pom on his way to Aus on P&O.

The staff had no idea who he really was, he was just another "resident" in God's waiting room. There was no time to chat about what he had done or achieved in his life, they were too busy.

He couldn't imagine that this was him for the rest of his life, so he'd better get a jog on and get himself going. George was eager to get started and was delighted to be introduced to Dorothy, a lovely friendly lady who gave him a big smile offered him a hug.

"Right let's get started" she announced enthusiastically, George was already feeling more motivated, and his spirits soared anticipating a renewed interest in life. It had never crossed his mind just how low in mood he was, but he certainly felt invigorated. Dorothy introduced him to the laptop and showed him how to do a search on Google, wow how amazing is that! The World Wide Web certainly opened his eyes!

"We'll start by setting you up with an email address, most people have an email address these days. Letters by post, it's known as snail mail because it's that slow. Email is quick and convenient, also you can deal with official things this way. You'll need a username and password, any ideas? usually it can be your name with something that makes it unique because there'll be millions of Georges."

"Erm … not like this George there won't."

"Well, tell me what's unique about you."

"I was a Grenadier Guard for many years, a bit of a ladies man you might say, I love playing chess, and rugby, well I did!"

"Mmm, Grenadier George, what year were you born?"

"1950" he smiled, "Many moons ago".

"So GrenadierGeorge50@gmail.com"

"Erm... GorgeousGrenadierGeorge50@gmail.com" sounds better, he laughed.

You can use this tablet for the time being, while you're learning. It will help you to have a practice. I'll send an email to you so I can check it's working. Ping ...

From Dorothydfairhurst65@gmail.com

Hi George,

Testing ... Testing

x Dorothy

"Exciting, you are now in the 21st century George, you have an electronic address!" remarked Dorothy. Click on the arrow and reply please so I can see you've got it.

"So just explain Dorothy, how would I benefit from an email address? Asked George.

"Well, it will improve your communication channels at least, most Government departments use email and a lot of official bodies. It's quicker than "Snail Mail" as we call it ..."

From GorgeousGrenadierGeorge50@gmail.

Hi Dorothy,

I've cottoned on to this quite quick, don't you think?

Can you play chess?

X Gorgeous George

(PS you're not bad yourself) Ha!

Ping ...

Dorothy glanced down "was that ping was your email landing George?"

"Have you read it?" he winked.

"Well, I know it's landed, that's the main thing, I'll open it after and check you've set it out ok."

"Does that mean I can get a pen pal?" That was one of my favourite things in my youth, especially when I was posted away from home."

"Yes maybe"

He thanked Dorothy for her time, it had made his afternoon. He secretly thought she would be a great catch but didn't want to scare her off, especially as she had to stay professional, she might give him a flea in his ear! Dorothy really got his heart racing, her perfume lingered around his seat in the lounge for hours after she left.

"I'll be back in next week, and excuse me for saying but, I bet you wink at all the girls!" waved Dorothy as she walked through the door. He watched as she got in her car and drove off. There was a glint in his eye for the rest of the day accompanied by a feeling of renewed hope.

George started thinking, as he wondered how having an email address might be useful to him, Dorothy hinted it would open many doors for me, he thought. He hoped that he would soon be well enough to go home, he wasn't ready for sitting on the settee in God's waiting room … just yet. That last chapter may still be possible if I play my cards right! George was eager to have a surf of the web and excitedly put in the search bar … pen pals, meet others then he added … for older people … click.

He was astonished how quick it was, it was a feast to the eyes, first real smile in ages …

Senior Dating Sites Over 60 – Meet Singles Your Age … Silver Singles

View your Matches for Free … provides a great chance for the elderly to socialise, particularly the more introverted.

His mind was working overtime, maybe my bucket list is still live after all, here's me thinking where would I meet someone at my age? Plenty of Fish?

Plenty of dinosaurs I'd say Lol ... He wondered what his niece would think, it seemed she had forgotten he existed, turned up now and seldom. Maybe she thought he'd really gone to seed and all that was needed was to wait for the will reading. Little did she know he wasn't ready to hand over his fortune just yet, what a surprise it would be to get an email from God's waiting room, a wry smile emerged as he started to hatch a plan.

The next day he was eager to see Helen and tell her about his session with Dorothy.

"It's like physio for the mind!" he enthused, "I've been looking how to get a pen pal, do you think you could help me to get on it, it's asking me all sorts of stuff & I'll need a photo and I'm not up to that yet, Lol"?

Helen laughed, she could see how much brighter George was, it was like someone had switched the light on.

Ping ... George had mail ...

From Dorothydfairhurst65@gmail.com

Good morning, George,

I've just read your email, Well done!

I do play chess and thanks for the compliment Cheeky!

I'll see you next week.   xx Dorothy

Helen noticed his eyes light up …

"Well Helen, can you help me to sort this Pen Pal thing out, they need a photo, phew, I'd better tidy myself up a bit. I think a collar and tie, and shave might help."

George was getting stronger each day and now had a renewed vision of getting home. Joyce, the physio turned up just as he was getting ready, there was a look of curiosity on her face,

 "All dressed up George?"

"And no-where to go" he quipped … "I'm doing really well, so let's get on with my exercises, I've got things to do."

Helen and Joyce looked at each other and laughed. It was the quickest session ever; it was obvious to Joyce that he was improving day on day.

He was eager to get his picture sorted so he could get going. Helen was expert at setting up profiles online, so it was a cinch to her. She soon had him shaved and dressed sat regally in his chair looking very dapper.

"Smile" , "You're on candid camera" replied George laughing, "I bet you've no idea what I'm on about." "Absolutely correct, and by the way, I've put a filter on this picture to cover some of your laughter lines. George roared laughing, "well those lines tell a great story, if you look closely."

"Now you can look at your matches, see this lady here, Lily, she's after a pen pal, she looks nice, mind you, be careful you don't start arranging dates, you have to walk before you can run you know."

George was clicking through at a pace. Like a child in a toffee shop! He looked through his matches and came across:

MissSFeckey1955@gmail.com Retired Secretary, all in blue, lovely face,

"Real lady seeks a gentleman for exchange of letters (email) initially, maybe open to meeting at a local group … eventually. In the first instance send introductory message."

… and a Miss too, twit twoooo!"

I'm going to take the plunge, it's now or never …

From GeorgeousGrenadierGeorge@gmail.com

Good afternoon, Sylvia, I'm delighted to see that you and I are a match so hello! You look like a very lovely lady, you have gorgeous eyes and a beautiful smile, can we converse, I'm a bit of an old-fashioned guy, I like to open doors for ladies and woo them with chocolates and flowers. Am I the guy for you?

Best wishes George x

A sense of accomplishment overcame him as he and Sylvia were chatting away, he told a little white lie telling her he was away just now in Australia visiting his niece but was hoping to be back in the next few weeks. Maybe they could talk on the phone sometime. She believed him when he said he had left his old Nokia Phone back home in UK. George became an expert at "This email lark" as he told Dorothy when she arrived the following week.

The enthusiasm was brimming over, he hardly drew breath, mind you, he had been looking forward to the vision of DD walking in, it made him all unnecessary!

"I've signed up for online dating, well emailing, I've got a pen-pal now, she's called Sylvia, she's really nice, we talk on the email all the time, it's like I've known her all my life, she's local ...." Words were spilling out like a dancing fountain.

"This Silver online group also organise local meeting places for members, you never know, Sylvia might be the Love of My Life, well the rest of my life."

"Have you been injected with a gramophone needle George?" smiled Dorothy, resting her gaze onto his face. He could feel his temperature rising, probably his blood pressure too, as they momentarily locked eyes. He tried to stay on plan,

"What a lovely dress Dorothy, and I have to say the hairdresser did a great job! Erm … It's just like old times this writing, it's like a modern letter, and I don't even need to wait for the postie, thank-you so much Dorothy, you've really opened a door for me."

"They also organise local meeting places for members, you never know, Sylvia might be the Love of My Life, well the rest of my life, that's once I can escape from here. However, I have to confess, I told Sylvia that I'm away in Australia, I don't want her knowing I'm stuck here just now."

"Don't be too hasty, as they say, plenty of fish, she might be a Sprat, but you never know when you might catch a Mackerel" Dorothy smiled. She was keen to introduce the local U3A, a group for over fifty-five's University of the Third Age".

"I know, don't get carried away, I get it."

Dorothy reassured George that soon, he would be fit enough to go home to his retirement apartment once he full got his strength back. He winked and nodded in agreement.

"You're great love, I can't tell you how much you've helped me, and it comes easier for me every day … surfing. I love it when you turn up! I've looked up all sorts of stuff and I feel confident with it, I know I'm not an expert, but who would be so soon?"

They chatted, Dorothy seemed to have the knack of lifting him, he seemed to have a feeling of renewed resolve each time he saw her. Sadness welled up inside at the prospect, of losing touch when he was discharged, she was such an inspiration! He thought of Sylvia too, they were really getting on well and, there were more matches he hadn't even looked at yet. He smiled as he remembered that Dorothy had reminded him that you catch a lot of Sprats before you get the Mackerel!

The days became a bit more purposeful for George as he became more mobile, he started helping the girls give out the cups of tea in the afternoon and joined in some of the activities. They were delighted to listen to George's tales of his list of lady penfriends. To his delight on the next Dr's visit, he was given permission to go home. George had plans, he would explore the possibility of meeting a partner, after all never say never, he thought. He emailed Dorothy and told her that with her help, having recovered well, he would be leaving the Grange the next day.

It was almost as if he'd never been away as he found himself looking out of his lounge window,

He felt lost without his connection to the www and quickly invested in getting online at home. He hadn't decided when he would break the news to Sylvia that he was home because she had been speaking of meeting when he returned from Australia. He wasn't sure he was ready just yet, so he might stay down-under for a little while.

He was impressed with the strapline when he Googled U3A … Learn, Live, Laugh. He was a bit nervous about walking into a meeting of strangers. It wasn't a bit like that, he had hardly set foot on the drive of the church when he heard the thong of chatting. George felt the aura of friendship as he approached and was accosted by middle-aged lady who breezed over, greeted him gushingly, and shepherded him inside. He was soon part of the group and returned home having signed up for walking group and local history.

I must tell Dorothy, he thought, and tapping away on his laptop, he emailed her …

From GorgeousGrenadierGeorge@gmail.com

Hi Dorothy,

Hope you're well and this email finds you on top of the world! I went to Upholland U3A today, what a friendly bunch. They had me signed up in no time! Walking & Local history. Settling in at home and feeling stronger every day. Missing our sessions, I still have a lot to learn when it comes to this surfing lark Lol! Still talking to Sylvia but she's a bit eager to meet now. There were some lovely ladies at the U3A, a few sprats as you might call them.

So …. Still looking for the love of my life

XX GGG

Ping … George eagerly opened the mail …

From Dorothydfairhurst@gmail.com

Hello George,

Nice to hear from you. Had a few busy weeks, good to hear you're doing well. You make me laugh you know, U3A member now, surfing, whatever next. I enjoyed our sessions too, your great company …

Ps The love of my life is down under, Lol

XX Dotty

Then it dawned …… Down Under, I wonder?

Be Careful What You Wish For

Many years ago, I got a new job with the title of Industrial Nurse. It involved looking after the employees of a company that manufactured mining equipment. I was pleased with the chance to work somewhere different; the added bonus was that it was local, only fifteen minutes' drive from home.

Unfortunately, there was not much of an induction process. My predecessor had worked there for donkeys any years but had sadly recently passed away. The employees were understandably in shock, so I was left to do what I could. The surgery was old fashioned and a mess, piles of Mills and Boone books adorned the floor and the sink in my office was hanging from the wall. I viewed it all with a positive attitude and knew I could change things for the better.

I quickly settled in and completed the backlog of medicals, I also got to know some of the workers, mainly the accident prone and the shirkers. The weeks rolled on and I thought of exciting improvements for the surgery and employees. I broached the subject with my boss and was told to leave it for a few months. One the first aiders told me that production is king in this business, the big bosses were not interested in the health of employees. I realised that this was the culture of the company, how could I change that?

In the New Year I had a couple of days sick, on returning to work, I was subjected to a few lewd comments and laughs as I walked past a group of workers on their lunch break. I ignored it, but over the next few days this childish behaviour continued. I asked one of the first aiders if he knew anything, he said there was a rumour that I had taken a few days sick leave due to being caught in an uncompromising position in the surgery with an employee. How pathetic, grown men spreading untrue rumours about the one woman who could help them if they were sick or injured. Later that week I had a couple of abusive phone calls in the surgery about the same subject. The factory doctor just told me to ignore it. I told my boss, and she said if it happened again, she would inform the police. By the following week I was yesterday's news, thankfully I carried on with my job.

After a few months I began to feel bored, each new idea I suggested was rejected, so I gave up. One day whilst reading the Nursing Times magazine I saw an advert for nurses to work on a cruise ship.

My day dreaming was in overdrive, Miss impulsive is my middle name so I decided to apply. Work life became easier as I had a plan, I was looking after myself, every day I felt excited to go home and discover if I had a letter about an interview. The following week my Mum was waving a letter around as I stepped through the door. Soon after that I was on a train to London for an interview.

My Mum accompanied my, she had already got a cruise brochure from the local travel agent, she was as excited as me at the adventure we were on. We found the hotel easily; the interview wasn't difficult, and I was in hight spirits as we enjoyed the rest of our day. Time flew by as we went shopping, site seeing and enjoyed a lovely lunch. It was a sunny day in mid-June, and I felt glad to be alive.

A couple of weeks later I received the news I had been waiting for, I had been successful, my dream had come true. At the beginning of July, I handed in my months' notice at the factory, my boss said she was shocked and saddened as the nurse did not usually leave. I didn't care and felt euphoric as the rumour quickly went around. Several of the employees came to the surgery to ask if the rumour was true, they could tell by my face that it was. The rest of the month passed by in a blur. A male nurse was employed on a short-term contract, I helped him to integrate as much as I could, this helped to smooth the transition process. A lot of the employees did not like this, they had expected a female nurse, they had always had female nurses. This was one change brought in that I couldn't take the credit for. I was also pleased to leave my safety shoes behind; they looked like I had borrowed them from Minnie Mouse.

On my final day I felt a bit sad, I had met some good people and become used to the role, however I knew that if I didn't take this chance, I would regret it for the rest of my life. The following week I flew to New York, the plan was to stay in the city overnight and to take a taxi to the ship the next day. I met a girl called Debbie in the hotel, she invited me for dinner with some of her friends, I was thrilled. I arrived at the hotel lobby at the pre-arranged time, nobody was there. I waited for ten minutes, no one came. I asked at reception and was informed that the group had already left. I was taken aback as I had trusted Debbie, I decided to strengthen my resolve and went out for dinner alone.

The next day I took a taxi to the cruise ship terminal, I met my colleague Heather, she was from Australia and had previously worked on two other cruise ships. We had to share a small cabin in the medical centre, however I had no time to dwell on this as there was work to be done. This involved meeting the passengers and answering any questions. This was difficult as I was new on the ship myself. I watched nervously as Heather worked her way around the passengers. She was telling me bits of information as I followed her. I tried to remember everything but felt overwhelmed. Later we went to the medical centre and Heather talked me through the regime. The cruise ship was from an American line and was for American passengers. I had to become proficient with the payment system also.

Suddenly the ship started to move, sail away had begun, we were on our way to Bermuda. We took the chance to go on deck for this, it was exciting to see the passengers happy, but I also had to remember that I wasn't one of them. We had lunch with the two doctors who were part of the team, Christian was from Belgium and Marco was Spanish. They had both worked on the ship before. The rest of the day passed by in a blur, I had never walked up and down as many stairs before, as I lived in a bungalow at home.

Next day we were on duty at 7:00am, our first task was to check the PH levels in the pools. I did not think was in the remit of a cruise ship nurse, but I kept quiet. The next hour was spent triaging any crew members who needed to be seen. Most of them spoke only basic English, we had to decide if we could fix their problem, or they needed to see the doctor. The next two hours were for any passengers, a big crowd appeared, and they did not seem to know how to queue. Several of them were shouting out what they wanted at the same time. The situation seemed crazy, I also had to remember to charge them for every item used. Although Heather was busy, she appeared to be there one minute and gone the next, I realised I needed to toughen up.

In the afternoon we had a couple of quiet hours, this was spent cleaning and restocking the medical room. At 4:00pm it was time for the crew clinic again, followed by the passengers. This appeared less hurried, Heather said this would change when we reached Bermuda as there were always a lot of accidents to deal with.

Reports of the number of people seen and quantity of money generated had to be on the staff captains' desk by 7:00pm. This was followed by testing the PH levels on the pools again. My head finally hit the pillow three hours later, I quickly fell asleep only to be woken twice in the night by the telephone ringing, Heather was on call she explained that it would be my turn soon. At the interview this was the doctor's remit, I felt too tired to think.

Overnight we had docked in Bermuda, excitement fizzed through me, I couldn't wait to get ashore as I had a free day. I met Christian at breakfast, he said he was going to the beach with friends, I hoped he would invite me too, but he did not. Heathers plan was to see her boyfriend. I explored the small port where we had docked. Sitting on bench staring at the glistening ocean, I realised that I wanted to go home.

Back onboard I explained my decision to Heather, she said she would ring the London office, I packed my suitcase feeling much better. Later that day we had a staff lifeboat drill, I had to climb down narrow stairs to the engine room. One man role played the patient that had to be lifted up the narrow stairs on a stretcher and carried to the medical room. Whilst there a siren sounded, we had to go to deck five, stand in a line wearing lifejackets. The staff captain inspected us, as he approached me, he pulled at the strings of my lifejacket and shook me like a rag doll, shouting "your lifejacket is loose." Then he turned his attention to the lady next to me, I smiled as I knew I would not go through that again.

I received a call from the woman who had interviewed me in London, her first words were, "what is wrong with you?" In a condescending tone, I told her exactly how I had found my experience. She had failed to mention about being on call, and had painted a fantastic job, just as I had when I daydreamed. We agreed I would leave the ship when we docked in New York in a few days' time. This was after I had vowed to send my story to the nursing times.

The next few days were bearable, when we docked in New York staff at the reception desk told me to return later. I decided to sit on my suitcase in the middle of the room until help arrived. This caused a stir especially with new passengers arriving. I was quickly despatched, pay cheque in hand onto the dockside.

At the airport I rang home and explained the situation to my dad, Oh God was his reply. Then he said he was proud of me and would see me soon.

At home I had to decide what I really wanted to do. My auntie suggested I contacted my ex-boss and ask for my job back. At first, I did not want to do this, however after a while it made sense as I knew I could do the job.

I made the call and went for an interview, I told them why I had left the company in the first place, they understood and agreed to take me back, the doctor I had worked with also agreed, I resumed my role at the factory six weeks later, news of my return quickly spread through the factory. I walked through the shopfloor to the sound of the men singing "We are Sailing." I laughed and knew I was back where I belonged.

The last Goodbye

"Please show your boarding passes and passports and prepare for boarding at gate 35, Alicante to Manchester," came a very efficient voice over the loudspeaker.

Amelia watched as a crowd of passengers rushed to the desk to board the plane all enthusiastic and chattering to each other. How could they be so happy when she felt so sad? She noticed some passengers showing off varying shades of sunburn in strappy tops and shorts, their hand luggage bulging with souvenirs and duty free, a mother soothing a small baby and a couple of businessmen in smart suits firmly attached to their brief cases and their noses stuck in their phones and an elderly gentleman in a wheelchair who was being assisted by a young member of staff.

As the queue died down Amelia approached the check in desk, her heart was heavy, and she had a feeling of impending doom. She had just left her parents villa. Mum was terminally ill, and Dad was doing his best to care for her, with alternate visits from Amelia and her sister Lucy who were both trained nurses. The health service in Spain was very different to the NHS in England and Mum refused to go to the hospital. Living in Spain had been paradise for her parents for the last twenty years, but it wasn't paradise now that they were elderly, and Mum was ill!

Amelia hadn't wanted to leave as she knew Mum's condition had deteriorated slightly, but she was supposed to be working tomorrow and she knew when the worst happened, she would need time off. So, she'd plastered a smile on her face, hugged Mum, and Dad, said goodbye and promised that she would be back soon. Whilst waiting in the airport, she had time to think and planned to speak to her manager the following day to arrange special leave and go back, for however long she was needed. Meanwhile, her sister Lucy was on her way from Manchester to take her turn.

Amelia boarded the plane and took her seat," great," she was in the middle seat, between a young Spanish man who greeted her politely and then gazed out of the window and a very large lady on the aisle seat who took up half of Amelia's seat as well! Oh well, it was only for three hours, and she would soon be home, where her husband Joe would be waiting for her. Unfortunately, events took an unexpected turn!

After about an hour, nothing had happened, the air hostesses seemed to be struggling with the cabin door and it was very hot. The smiling passengers were no longer smiling and getting irritable. The captain appeared at the doorway to the cockpit and in a very defeated tone informed the passengers that they would have to disembark as one of the baggage handlers had damaged the cabin door when he has thrown a case on board. They would now have to wait for a new door part to arrive from England!

Once back in the terminal, meal vouchers were issued and then frustratingly the staff seemed to disappear. Amelia had made phone calls to Joe to tell him she had been delayed and to work to say she wouldn't be home in time for her shift! That didn't go down well!
She noticed that the elderly gentleman in the wheelchair was panicking and was slightly annoyed that no one was helping him, so she took matters into her own hands as she would have hoped that someone would have helped her parents, if they had needed it. She discovered that his name was Eric and that he was partially sighted. She helped him to phone his son and promised to make sure he was kept safe. By now, the rest of the passengers were restless and

agitated that they had been abandoned with no information! Amelia found a flight tracker on her phone and relayed updates to everyone else. She felt better keeping herself occupied. Next, she tracked down a member of staff at the help desk who said, "she was now off duty," but Amelia's firm, no nonsense approach made her contact a senior manager and the next minute, there was a message for the passengers to go to the bus stop outside the airport as they were being transferred to a hotel overnight and hopefully, their plane would be repaired by morning! The hotel was basic, but at least there was a bed and bathroom facilities.

On arrival, there was some confusion with the Spanish lady on reception, who initially spoke very good English. Amelia was assisting Eric with his travel documents and the receptionist suggested they share a room and was surprised when she Amelia declined. Amelia tried to explain that they had just met at the airport, but the receptionist suddenly only spoke Spanish and didn't seem to understand, until the Spanish gentleman, she'd been sat next to on the plane came to her rescue and explained in a very animated fashion what had happened. Amelia was very grateful for his support and happy when she managed to get a room to herself. She'd had enough for one day and just wanted to be alone.

It was a long night, Amelia was restless, she couldn't sleep, she was running on adrenaline and in limbo at the same time. She was fearful of oversleeping and missing the coach back to the airport in the morning and she had plenty of time to worry about Mum and how Dad would cope on his own in Spain, when Mum inevitably passed away.

In the morning, Amelia was exhausted but relieved to catch the coach back to the airport. She grabbed a coffee and made her way back to the departure gate, praying that this time they would get home.

Whilst waiting to board at around nine o clock, she rang Dad and Lucy, who reported, "that Mum was looking a little better this morning." Amelia updated them on the delay saga and promised that she would be back soon. Fatigue had set in now, but Amelia couldn't sleep on the plane as she was squashed and uncomfortable. She longed for her own bed and promised herself that she would sleep before ringing her manager later.
Joe met her warmly at the arrivals gate. Amelia melted into his strong arms before he took her hand luggage and ushered her into the car. Amelia accepted his offer of to go for lunch on the way home and felt better after they had eaten.

It was late afternoon and they had just got home and settled down with a cup of tea when Amelia's phone rang. It was Lucy! "You need to come back as soon as you can, "cried Lucy. "Mums just passed away and me and Dad need you." Amelia's world crashed around her. She felt numb with shock, even though they had all known that this would happen eventually, she couldn't believe what she was hearing as Dad and Lucy had said that Mum had seemed better six hours ago! If only she had known, yesterday that it would be her last goodbye, she would never have left the villa. It was too late now but she wished with all her heart that she could rewind the last twenty-four hours and spend the precious time with mum.

Through floods of tears, she moved from Joe's strong, comforting embrace and reached for her laptop to book the next flight back to Spain for her and Joe.

The Surprise

As she replenishes the stock in the shop window Pauline looks out at the scene on the pavement outside the row of shops. It's rather like snapshots of life unfolding before her. Mothers hurrying children towards school, the older ladies deep in conversation having a good gossip and often someone who's just used the cashpoint studying their mini statement, their expressions inscrutable, is it good news or bad? She'd never have dreamt when she first started at the shop the shock she'd have when she discovered the secrets about her own family.

The voluntary job that she has in the charity shop is so different from her previous career in finance, no pressure or deadlines, no career ladder to be attempted and no poisonous office politics. When the decision to return to her home village had to be contemplated it was far easier than she's have imagined, if someone had asked her five or ten years earlier if she'd be happy to give up her city life and career to go back to care for her failing Mother she'd have said that she'd do it but feel conflicted about it. She'd loved the social life and cut & thrust of the business but in recent years it had lost its appeal.

Pauline had done well at school, excelled in some subjects much to everyone's - especially her own – surprise. In retrospect she thought that she'd concentrated her efforts on her schoolwork as a diversion from her home life, though happy she'd always sensed the undercurrent of tension between her parents. Her Mother had always appeared to have an underlying grudge against her father and there was an atmosphere in the house when they were both there. As a child when Pauline commented on how smart he looked in his army uniform on the photograph of the two of them taken after his passing out parade she'd made a derogatory comment 'he thought he was somebody in those days', it was as though she somehow resented her commenting that he looked good in his uniform.

When she'd decided to go into the sixth form instead of getting a job there'd been raised eyebrows at home. Her Father was just surprised & though her mother didn't object she thought that further educations was wasted on women, it was a generation thing, in her day women worked until they married, had a child and were housewives from then on. The wish to go to university surprised her parents even more but they were supportive and gave her both encouragement and financial support which she was very grateful for. Her university years were a revelation in so many ways, living away from home in a city, managing money, cooking for herself, doing her own laundry but also the freedom to come and go as she wished, no deadlines for when to be home – in fact depending on who she met she sometimes stayed out all night. Of course, she looked for a job in the city after she finished her business degree, the best jobs were there & once she'd had a taste of city life returning to her home village and living with her parents held no appeal. She soon got a job with a firm of accountants and moved into a rented flat; the world was her oyster.

There were of course encounters with men, some became boyfriends, but she never felt that she wanted a long-term commitment. She enjoyed their company and the physical side of the relationships, but she didn't wish to live with them or make the situation permanent. Whether this was a result of what she'd seen of her parents' relationship or the desire to be a focused career woman she didn't know. Her outings with female friends and colleagues were really some of her best times, her social life was full, and she didn't feel that she was missing out by not having a husband or children.

It was almost ten years now since her father had died, he'd seemed well but had started with severe stomach pains, the ambulance took him to hospital but there was nothing that could be done, he'd had an aortic aneurysm that had ruptured. The visits home became more frequent once her mother was alone, she'd always gone to visit every six weeks but that changed to every three weeks or so. the surprising thing was that she started to feel more relaxed when she was there, the pressures of work were trying and now that she'd got into her fifties the city held less appeal.

She'd moved back home when her mother began to struggle with failing health, financially she was fine, she sold the flat that she'd bought several years before & moved back into her childhood home, it was easier to provide care there. It was only a couple of years later that her mother had a massive stoke and died, it was a shock at the end, and she missed her more than she'd expected to.

After the funeral she was immersed for quite a while in sorting out her mother's affairs, it seemed never ending the phone calls to insurance companies and sorting out the bits of paperwork. Eventually the last of the loose ends were tied up and she had time to herself. At first, she enjoyed the freedom of having little to do and spent plenty of time reading and gardening plus sorting the bungalow to her own specifications. When the autumn came, she started to find herself with too much time to fill and started to feel a little down, she really needed to find something to do where she was mixing with people. One cool and breezy afternoon as she walked to the supermarket, she noticed a sign in the charity shop 'volunteers needed,' she paused for a second and then continued her journey. Later that evening Pauline sat thinking about the sign in the shop window, it could be a good way to use her time in many ways, she'd be helping a good cause, getting out and meeting people, the decision was made. The following day she went into the shop and had a chat with the lady in charge, it went well, and she started working the following week. Her days were Tuesday and Wednesday, she soon got used to the way things were done and loved working there. Unlike her professional career there was no pressure and she found that she really enjoyed the interaction both with the staff and the customers. She'd never given much thought as to the clientele of a charity shop and she had a bit of an eye opener, if she'd been asked before she started there, she'd have said that most of the customers were down on their luck, the stock tatty and old fashioned. That wasn't the case at all, there were customers from all sorts of backgrounds, indeed there were the down at luck ones but also Mums with small children who donated outgrown stuff and purchased bigger sizes, working men and women who just something new to wear and older folk who were often fancying a new cardi but often ended up with an ornament instead. The fact that there would be 'regulars' hadn't occurred to her either, people who were in several times a week having a mooch but also looking for a chat, most of these were older people. Pauline was happy to chat to anyone and soon got to know the regulars quite well.

One of the regulars, Betty was very chatty, and she looked forward to their chats. On one of the first occasions that they spoke she noticed that her accent wasn't local and when she mentioned it was clear why Betty came in the shop so regularly for a natter. Betty told her that she'd been born and brought up in a small town in Yorkshire where her father was the bank manager, she'd been bright at school, and he pulled strings to get her a job in the branch when she left school. It was classed as a good job for a woman in those days when most girls went straight from school into the mill. As time went on Betty revealed a bit more about her life and Pauline was interested but sometimes felt that she was prying, as much as Betty loved a chat, she sometimes seemed reticent to talk about her past. Apparently, she'd moved to this area in the 1950's due to a slight job promotion, but that seemed a strange thing to do in those days as a single woman when people often lived in the same street all their lives.

By early on the Wednesday afternoon Pauline started to get uneasy about Betty not having been into the shop. Like most elderly ladies she was a creature of habit and always came in quite early in the day, what made it more significant was that she'd been in the day before and said that she'd forgotten to pick up a bag of stuff that she was bringing in for them to sell and as she left she said she said that she'd be back in the morning with it. It played on her mind, as much as Betty was in her eighty's she was very sharp mentally and wouldn't have forgotten. When she left the shop at the end of the day, she decided that she would call on Betty on her way home, she knew where she lived as she'd once been to collect a large mirror that Betty had donated and was too heavy for her to carry to the shop.

As she pulled up at the front of the house Pauline noticed that there were no lights showing inside, it wasn't quite dark, but the light had started to fade so it would be quite dark inside, she'd have thought that there'd be at least one window showing a light. She rang the bell twice & there was no answer then knocked at the front door in case the bell was broken but still no answer.

Through the frosted glass of the door, she thought that she could see Betty's walking stick propped up against the wall, she'd never seen her out without it and that convinced her that she must be in the house. To the left of the door was the lounge window and when she looked through there, she thought that she could see the top of someone's head above the back of the armchair that was under the window. With no more ado Pauline tried the front door, it was unlocked, she entered the hallway and called Betty's name. After a couple, more attempts at shouting she went into the lounge. Through the glom she could see Betty sat in the chair, she had obviously passed away suddenly and peacefully, she just looked as though she had fallen asleep.

Shocked and saddened as she was, she knew that she'd have to make a phone call, she knew that in such circumstances you called 999 and they would advise what to do. She turned on the light & made the call her voice and hands trembling. Turning around to where Betty sat, she walked across to say a little prayer before she was taken away, Pauline was a lapsed Catholic but what had been ingrained in her childhood had stuck with her through the years and it was what she felt that she must do now. The words of the prayers were easy to recall, and she said the words aloud, as she did her eyes went to a table at the side of the chair, on it were a couple of ornaments and a black and white photograph in a frame.

Pauline looked at the photograph and moved closer to study it, her heart banged in her chest, the shock of finding someone dead was bad enough, but nothing could have prepared her for this. The smiling couple on the photograph were her father in his army uniform and Betty, they were under the jawbone arch in Whitby. As she waited for emergency services to arrive her head was whirling with questions and thoughts.

Had her mother known about her father's affair and that's why she was so resentful towards him?

Did Betty move here because she knew that it was where her father lived and she hoped to rekindle the affair, could the affair have been rekindled and that was why she was here?

More than anything Pauline wondered if Betty had known who she was, that would explain her reticence when asked about her past, could her visits to the shop & chats been in some way her way of forming a link to her father?

The truth was that Pauline would never have the answers that she craved to these questions, the puzzle would never be solved.

She picked up the photograph & went outside to await the ambulance.

RESCUED

Our beautiful dog Kelly joined our family in an untraditional way. My partner and I decided to buy a golden retriever puppy for our four children, who were recovering from broken marriages on both sides of the family. The children were all feeling unsure and bewildered, each sensing they had lost their familiar position within their family units. After some discussion between ourselves, we decided that a puppy would be just the thing to help bond our new family together.

A neighbour quickly informed us that a golden retriever on our estate had just been delivered of ten puppies. After making a few enquiries we arranged to go and view them. Kelly was a perfect specimen of the Golden Retriever breed. Her coat was silky and amber gold in colour, and longer than average length. However, her eyes told another story, she was both sad, and worried at the predicament she found herself in. Her tail was tucked so far between her legs it was hardly visible. Having to protect her litter made Kelly cautious and suspicious of us. We were welcomed by a low throaty growl, as she warned us not to touch her babies.

The owner led us slowly down the hallway towards her. She looked back over her shoulder remarking as she did so,

"Can you wait a moment while I separate the pups from her. She's very protective and vicious with anyone who tries to touch them."

To my horror she brought out a long wooden broom handle which supported a homemade wire noose at one end. She deftly snared Kelly's muzzle with the noose and dragged her away. Once the mother was safely out of the room, I eagerly peered into the whelping box, only to see ten completely black mongrel puppies. My heart sank, I was unable to hide my feelings,

Showing my disappointment I exclaimed, "Oh we don't want a mongrel, I didn't realise they weren't pedigrees."

Kelly's owner seemed more than a little put out by my obvious rejection, and she apologised for wasting our time, so much so, I felt obliged to explain.

"I'm sorry, but we really want a golden retriever, the whole family has set their heart on having one," with tongue in cheek I said, "if you want to give us the mother, we would be happy to take her off your hands."

Never dreaming what would happen next. My second shock of the day was the reply she gave,

"You can have her if you want her, I'm taking them all to the dogs home next week, I'm sick of them all, when can you take her?"

I just couldn't believe our good fortune, still reeling from the surprise, we arranged to pick Kelly up the following week, complete with her pedigree which to be honest, was extremely fine indeed. Her pedigree name was Laurel Hampton Gay Lady and boy didn't she know it! She always got her own way, and was treated like the lady she was, for the rest of her life. So that is how she started her new life with us.

Kelly was about fourteen months old when we adopted her. She had already had two previous owners in her short lifetime and was poorly trained, disobedient, and quite vicious too. Once she moved in with us, we realised that she was literally starving, Kelly had not been fed properly or given any supplements at all during her pregnancy or after the birth of her puppies. As a result of feeding them all herself, she was grossly underweight, in fact, half the weight she should have been. Her ribs were protruding through her fur and her teats almost dragging on the floor.

We decided to take her to the vets for a check-up, and were not surprised to learn she needed injections, antibiotics for severe mastitis, vitamins and much more besides. It took several months to restore her to the beautiful dog we remember so well. We found out later that during her puppy days, she was beaten with a garden spade, frightened with bangers tied to her tail, and teased unmercifully by her first owners who popped crisp bags, and opened beer cans near her ears and nose. She never quite overcame her fear of pops and bangs and always spent bonfire night sitting in the bathtub. I don't know why she did this, but every year it was the same.

People say animals soon forget, but I beg to differ, whenever Kelly approached the gate of her previous owner, she either ran past it full pelt, or sat down before we even got there, putting her paw over the lead refusing to take one more step in that direction just in case she was being taken back there. So determined was she, that we literally had to drag her past the gate on her backside.

We also noticed that she never wagged her tail, it remained tightly between her legs for almost a year. After a lot of coaching, verbal commands, and by physically showing her how to wag it, she did finally respond, always obliging us with a quick flutter whenever we said, "Come on Kell wag your tail," Over time it became one of her best party tricks.

She also loved to collect toys, socks, slippers, storing a large pile of bric-a-brac in her basket. If anything went missing it was always the first place we looked, and we generally found it there. Being a retriever Kelly loved water and would swim for miles if given the chance. She loved her walks too, but it was not a relaxing past time for us, because we were continually on the lookout for ponds, ditches, and brooks into which she would gleefully leap at every opportunity. She became known as the swamp monster in our local neighbourhood because as a general rule, she returned home stinking to high heaven, covered in slime, mud and on occasions much worse. Thank goodness she was happy to continue having fun when she got home while we rinsed her off with the hosepipe. Kelly always accompanied us on our rambling club weekend walks too. On one particular occasion we had arranged to walk along the Leeds Liverpool canal in Wigan, of course she had to do her usual thing! At the first opportunity she dove into the canal and swam along its length for the complete section of our journey. My husband eventually managed to drag her out by her collar and front legs, she wasn't for getting out I can tell you.

Kelly did have one more dramatic event during her life with us. We decided to take the whole family including her on holiday to Norfolk for a week in a camper van. This was to lead to the only trauma Kelly experience with us. When we arrived at the beach, I wanted a bit of peace and quiet, and I decided to spend some down time in the sandhills, while the rest of the family played on the shore. Eventually I decided to join them on the sands, Kelly was nowhere to be found. Both my husband and I had assumed she was with the other. Suddenly I spotted her, a speck on the horizon. We were not aware at the time that this coastline was notorious for rip tides, and regularly dragged people out to sea, and Kelly too on this occasion. Fortunately, my husband Tony is a particularly good swimmer, and so without giving the situation another thought he swam out to get her. He told us later that when he finally reached Kelly, she was exhausted, whimpering, and terrified. As he approached her, he called out to her "Kelly, come on girl, get onto my back." Without a moment's hesitation she did so, gripping Tony's shoulders with her claws, desperately holding onto him. It took half an hour for him to swim to shore and Kelly cried and whimpered all the way back. In retrospect swimming out to rescue the dog was an extremely dangerous thing to do. Fortunately, all went well, although Tony bore the scars on his shoulders for quite a while afterwards. Kelly learnt her lesson that day and did not go near the sea again for the rest of the holiday.

In later life, Kelly developed breast cancer, which the vet thought was a result of the habitual beatings she had suffered as a puppy. Happily, she recovered well after having an operation to remove the tumour and lived for another three years after that. Kelly proved to be a very loyal loving friend to everyone in our family, including the cats, but she could not be trusted with people she did not know. She made every effort to bite the refuse collectors on a weekly basis. We knew in our hearts that she was grateful for the tender loving care she always received from us. We did eventually manage to change most of her bad habits, and after many years of coaxing, she learnt to carry a beer can across the room, but only for chocolate drops. She never got used to bangers, party poppers, Christmas crackers or the crinkle of crisp bags.

Kelly was the first dog I ever owned, and although we have had several others since, she will always have a special place in my heart.

Old Tin Box

As Jade placed her mobile phone on the table with a sigh Ian turned and asked who had been on the call.

Jade told him that her mum had been on the phone to say that her dad had pulled his back whilst on the allotment.

Apparently, he had been getting the base ready for the new shed which was due to be delivered by the end of the week.

"Ring your mum and tell her I will give him a few hours tomorrow and then we can settle down and watch the match." Said Ian, "It will stop your dad becoming all stressed and tell her to tell him he can supervise."

"I can help in the morning then take Mum shopping when the match is on." Said Jade relieved and gave him a peck on the cheek leaving a pink mark which Ian rubbed off smiling.

 The following morning, they all trouped down to the allotment where Tony sat on the old bench waiting to fulfil his role as supervisor.

"I can watch folk work all day" he laughed, sadly the comment only received a few tuts and eyes raised up to the heavens.

"Right, what do you want us to do first?" asked Ian.

"Well, the base is ready for the new shed, so ideally, I need the soil turning over where the old shed was. The foliage I cut down needs saving for Mrs Winstanley for the local flower arranging classes, I promised her I would save it for her."

Jade set about placing the greenery in the compost bags ready to place in the boot of the car, when later Mrs Winstanley suddenly appeared.

"I saw you all from my window coming down to the allotment earlier this morning so I thought I would bring you hot drinks and some of the cakes and pastries I bought at the Market yesterday. I thought you might need a little nourishment."

Ian's spade fell to the ground as he hurried over for the unexpected treat.

"Jade, your mum said not to rush getting back, she doesn't need anything urgently from the shops as she can use the things in the freezer that has been stock piling. Which I should do as I keep buying foods on offer and cramming them in the freezer heaven only knows what is in the back."

Jade agreed as she was also guilty of doing the same.

Mrs Winstanley poured out the hot drinks and offered the pastries and cakes which were taken quite gladly. Mrs Winstanley very rarely got her first name; this was due to her being the retired head teacher at the local school. In fact, there was only a hand full of people that could tell you her first name. She also gave swimming lessons to the school children at the local swimming pool on a Saturday morning.

Food eaten and drinks drank, the work commenced again. After a few minutes Ian called out that he had hit something hard like metal. They all grouped around to see what the object was. On lifting the object from the ground Tony said it was an old-fashioned metal cash box.

"Hidden treasure" squealed Jade in high hopes

"Bring it over here on the bench and let's see if we can open it" said Tony patting the spare place besides him.

The box was badly rusted and took some time to lever the lid from the bottom. Once opened there was a letter addressed to "The finder,"

Tony took the letter from the envelope carefully as the paper inside was delicate.

He read aloud. Dear Finder,

If you are reading this letter, it means I am dead.

Everyone gasped in unison. Tony raised his head to see Mrs Winstanley's hand go to her throat and turn quite pale.

Tony immediately told her to take a seat on the bench before she fainted, he was afraid she would head but the ground. After a few deep breaths Mrs Winstanley seemed to recover. He placed the old box on his knee and after looking at Jade and Ian continued to read on.

I did not kill my lovely Alice, I am innocent. The police are about to arrest me any minute as I cannot prove to them, I did not do it. Please, if possible, find her true killer.

I hope someday to clear my name and if not, you are reading this as I have been wrongfully arrested and done a life sentence for a crime I did not do. If my parents are still alive, please tell them I love them and would never kill anyone. Honestly, I wouldn't.

My heart is breaking knowing I will never again hold Alice in my arms or smell her lovely freshly washed brunette hair.

Yours Sincerely and in hopes,

Albert Lord.

Tony folded the fragile paper carefully and placed it back into the open box. For a few moments there was complete silence amongst the group until Mrs Winstanley said quite quietly.

"Albert Lord, now there is a name I haven't heard in donkeys' years. He did get arrested for Alice Hampson's murder many years ago and as I recall there were lots of rumours flying around saying he was being made a scape goat for someone else who had allegedly done the murder."

"Whose Murder would that be then?" asked Helen, Tony's wife, who was walking up to the huddled group, they hadn't until that moment seen her approaching.

"Oh, mum you need to read this letter we found in the old cash box, it is ever so sad." Said Jade, pointing to the box.

"Helen, do you remember a Boy called Albert Lord?" Enquired Mrs Winstanley. "He was jailed for the murder of Alice Hampson. They were both in the late teens, and everyone thought they were an ideal couple, so good looking the pair of them. She worked at Enfield mill, and he was a farmer's son."

"Yes, that name has catapulted me back years" replied Helen, "I do remember her hair, brunette long wavy and so shiny I would have given anything for hair like that. I also remember there being a lad who made himself a nuisance around that time, Jack Gray. It was thought that he was the murderer. Marjorie Moore said she had seen him earlier that night with Alice, when she was on her way to work at the Railway pub, but the police dismissed it as he had an alibi. His brother Frank swore to the police that Jack had been there with him most of the evening. Marjorie said she heard Frank calling Jack a bloody idiot after he had spoken in a very hushed voice. They both left hurriedly. The content of the speech was unknown."

Mrs Winstanley became quite excitable as she recounted events.

"Marjory told the police that Jack had indeed come into the pub where she was a part time barmaid. However, the time he gave, and the time Marjory gave the police was totally different. The Gray brothers had been bullies from an early age and it was thought the police themselves were feared of the whole family."

"What happened to the Jack fellow?" asked Ian.

"He participated in a robbery not long after Albert was jailed. As he fled from the building, he ran into the road and was hit by the number seven bus going to Abbey Lakes. It was said he died instantly." Said Mrs Winstanley. "Karma, that's what I would say wouldn't you?"

"And his brother Frank, What about him?" asked Jade

"I believe, he actually confessed when he was as drunk as a mop or up to the eyeballs with drugs in the pub one night, take your pick. The police were informed but he wasn't found for some time" said Mrs Winstanley soberly.

"Frank was eventually found drowned in a flooded quarry. It was said he was swimming whilst drunk. I think he was done in myself, and it would serve him right," said Helen.

"Does Albert have any living family?" asked Jade.

Mrs Winstanley paused in thought for a while trying her best to remain calm.

"Yes, there were two sisters, we were all very good friends, all went to the same school, grew up together," recalled Mrs Winstanley. "However, there is only one sister remaining. Her name is Ester, she is the youngest of the siblings. Ester lives near to me, and I see her quite regularly. In fact, Ester trained as the first lady bus driver, which was quite unheard of around here. Mrs Winstanley gave a little chuckle. "Ester fought hard for Alberts release," continued Mrs Winstanley, "unfortunately Albert died in jail. It was said he died of a broken heart. His name was cleared eventually when a member of the Gray family admitted to the police that Jack had indeed committed the murder, even though he had not intended to. Ester received a full pardon on Albert's behalf."

"I am pleased that Alberts name was finally cleared." said Jade clearly saddened. "What a tragic story."

The letter was placed back into the old tin cash box and given to Mrs Winstanley to do what she felt was the best.

Ester hurried to answer the impatient knocking on her front door, thinking she would give them a piece of her mind when she eventually got to open the door. Ester was troubled with arthritis in her right hip which caused her to be less agile as she was used to, and therefore slowed her down.

Ester opened the door to find Mrs Winstanley bent breathlessly holding herself up with one arm on the dividing wall and very puce in the face.

Ester guided her to her lounge and put Mrs Winstanley in the nearest easy chair.

"Good gracious Janice you get your breath while I get you a stiff drink" Ester said going to the cupboard where she kept her spirits (for medicinal purposes!)

Ester lifted out her favourite brand of whisky, Janice didn't raise an objection.

"Ester, it's your Burt" Janice manages to say in between gasps for her breath.

"He buried a box in Tony's Garden, and they came across it. When they opened it there was a letter inside"

Janice leaned over to get her bag and brought out the old tin box to which she held out to Ester.

Ester turned to pour out a second shot of whisky placed it on the coffee table then took the old box from Janice.

Reluctantly she opens the box to see the letter which she removed and opened it gingerly and read the writing her brother had written too many years ago.

A sob caught in her throat. The tears streamed down her face.

Janice went over to comfort her oldest and dearest friend.

"I didn't know about this, such a shock after all this time" Ester held the dirt covered box to her chest. "What was said when you were at Tony's?"

"Tony knew Burt's history, but he was a surprised at finding the box as we are, Jade wasn't aware of the house being your family home prior to them moving in."

Ester was quiet for moment sipping her whisky. The ticking mantle clock which hadn't been heard earlier now seemed deafening.

"I don't regret what I did to Jack" Ester said with a firm voice and looking directly at Janice.

"I don't regret what I did Frank, another few minutes he would have drowned anyway I just help him go a little quicker."

Ester refilled their glasses and raising them together both echoed "to Burt Rest in Peace."

Coming Home

The pre-war semi stood empty, it looked very forlorn and in need of a great deal of care and attention. In former days, the house would have looked majestic, standing there on the brow of the hill flanked by houses on either side. My fiancé and I were sitting together on an old garden bench almost hidden by the waist high grass at the rear of the property chatting happily. We had just agreed to the sale of the property and had signed and exchanged contracts. Although I felt excited about the purchase, I also felt sad for Mrs Winstanley, the elderly lady from whom we had bought the house. She had been forced to sell her home because her husband was ill in hospital. Visiting had proved difficult, as she travelled back and forth into the city every day to be at his bedside. As winter approached, she had decided to sell the house and move nearer to the hospital where he was being cared for. When we viewed the house Mrs. Winstanley had told us that her husband did not want her to sell it, but she had decided to go ahead anyway. She gave an explanation to justify herself saying, he wasn't the one having to travel on two buses every day in all weathers to see him.

Through the long winter evenings, we scraped sanded and painted the house from top to bottom, gradually transforming it back to its former glory. Old brown varnish giving way to brilliant white gloss, antiquated wall coverings, sometimes five layers thick, to airy patterns. Damp and mould disappearing as rooms yielded to fresh air and the temperate conditions of central heating. For six months we spent every spare moment in our first home. We gave little thought to Mrs Winstanley, other than to wonder how she had lived so long in such dirty dismal conditions. Two days before our wedding, every room gleamed like a new pin, we were settled, happy, and looking forward to our future together.

Shortly after our marriage, on a warm sunny Saturday afternoon, my husband had gone to play cricket for his local team while I had decided to stay at home and do a few household chores. I can clearly remember standing in the doorway of the master bedroom, looking out onto the landing. The sun was streaming in through the window, reflecting thousands of minute dust particles which made them look like a shower of golden rain. The brilliant white paintwork on the banister rail and wooden floorboards reflecting the light. The brass stair rods holding down the claret-coloured stair carpet shining like gold, casting spots of light upon the ceiling and walls. The atmosphere was magical, tranquil, and quite profound, my heart was full, and I felt totally at peace.

As I left the bedroom my jubilant mood deserted me. I was shocked to see a small elderly man of about seventy years of age standing on the landing to the left of me. He was wearing a brown checked flat cap, and a filthy beige trench coat buttoned up to the neck and belted haphazardly at the waist. The cuffs and collar of his coat were caked with dirt and looked greasy black in appearance. He was just under five feet in height, and weighed approximately eight stone, he had a pronounced hump on his back just below his left shoulder. His moon shaped face was dough-like in appearance and had a grey pallor. As he turned and looked at me, he had an expression of bewilderment on his face. My mind was racing, who was this man? how had he got into the house? what did he want? was he a burglar? questions filled my head, I could feel my heart pounding. I looked this little old man in the eye and calmly asked,

"What do you want – what are you doing here?"

Without hesitation he replied saying, "I've come home."

"This isn't your home, you don't live here now," I protested.

The old man looked around wistfully and replied sadly,

"I know, I can see that now"

As his final words tapered off, he turned his back on me and walked towards the sunlight and simply disappeared. Strange as it might seem, I did not feel afraid of the stranger once I had spoken to him, but after he had gone, I felt an overwhelming sadness for him.

For several minutes after this strange encounter, I did not move, but slowly it dawned on me that I had seen a ghost. Although I had never met Mr Winstanley, I knew with certainty that I had just spoken to him. Having regained my composure, I ran downstairs and went to speak to my elderly neighbour. She had lived next door to the Winstanley's for many years, I quickly related my experience to her, giving her a description of the man, I had seen. After listening to my tale, she said she was in no doubt whatsoever that my visitor had been Mr. Winstanley. She was amazed by the vivid description I had given her of her old neighbour. She explained that Mr Winstanley had for most of his working life, delivered coal to the local villagers and was a well-loved and a familiar figure throughout the neighbourhood, renowned for his flat cap and raincoat which he wore in all weathers while delivering his coal.

However, the story did not finish there, the week after my sighting, I received a brief note from Mrs. Winstanley telling me her husband had died on the previous Saturday afternoon. A slight chill ran down my spine as I read her news and realised that Mr. Winstanley had revisited his home on the day he passed away. Although it proved to be a sad experience, I'm glad to say my unexpected guest never visited again, and the years we lived in the house on the hill, hold some of my happiest memories.

The Dance

The cool spring breeze blew gently lifting the folds of Jean's full skirt, making her shiver

slightly as she tapped her feet as she waited patiently at the bus stop on the high street.

The chill early evening air pushing stray tendrils of her perfectly styled hair across her

cheeks. Steel grey clouds were gathering above threatening to unleash yet another spring shower.

"No not yet "muttered Jean as she huddled under the small bus shelter, as the first spots of rain started to patter on the tin roof above her, threatening to ruin her beautiful hair style. It had taken her hours to get her glossy auburn hair just right.

It's May 1945, life for Jean is pretty grim especially since dad came home from fighting in Africa with his left leg amputated at the knee and suffering from shell shock. Mum always a nervous woman is now a wreck living on cigarettes and coffee. She is constantly at dad's beck and call, running their little home in the sleepy backwater of Little Sudworth, and with her voluntary work with the WI on top of all that poor mum doesn't know whether she is coming or going just now. Jean's brother Jack still being stationed near Germany just makes things worse too, hopefully mum will feel better when he comes home. Jean hopes her brother will be home soon; apart from the effect it is having on mum Jean really misses him.

Jean runs her hands over her beautiful navy dress covered in white polka dots, smoothing out imaginary wrinkles from the gorgeous material. The dress fits snuggly over her bosom; Jean feels good; sexy even, although the fabric cost all her clothing coupons for the last six months; but it was worth it. She is confident, feels like a million dollars! Its cinched tight at her tiny waist with a full swinging skirt down to her knees; just perfect for dancing the night away. Sometimes Jean feels a bit selfish. She thinks of mum's sad face as she flounced out of the house tonight, after yet another row. Always about Jean going out but she tells herself that at 18 and after working hard in the sewing factory all week she deserves her one night out. Saturday night is the night for dancing, although she can still hear mums parting words echoing in her ears.

"Remember our Jeanie; those army boys are only after one thing and once you give in to them, they will leave you in trouble and bugger off back to war! So, keep your hand on your halfpenny and make sure you don't miss the last bus."

"Come on Dotty!" she mutters impatiently; her best friend since school and now work pal

Dotty is always late; but hey that is Dotty and Jean is used to her errant ways. That doesn't stop her from being frustrated though and she just hopes that Dotty gets there before the bus. Excitement is building by way of butterflies fluttering in her tummy made worse by the wait.

Jean gazes down the high street as she waits; her mind wandering as she notices the once bustling busy shops now mostly rubble after the blitz. All of the lovely dress and shoes shops where her and Dotty would spend their Saturday afternoons window shopping the trendy clothes and high heeled shoes. Now all gone, nothing but mess and chaos remaining in their place.

Her mind wanders back to the last time that she saw Him! It was over nine months ago now, the day before he and Jack were posted to Europe. Childhood friends Jack and Ken were inseparable and had joined up together as soon as they were able. Unlike her mum, who had been devastated when Jack decided to go and fight, Ken's mum was ever so proud of her son doing his bit for his country as she told everyone who would listen.

It had been a balmy late summer evening and Jean and Ken had only just officially started going steady even though they had known each other since Jean was a small girl; she had always loved Ken and was overjoyed when he had asked her mum if he could take her out properly. Ken had seemed nervous and apprehensive from the moment he had picked her up at home that evening; his eyes were dark and brooding and worry creased his brow; Jean assumed that he was nervous about the upcoming posting. He had taken her for a walk in the local park; said he needed to talk to her; that expression had set alarm bells ringing and Jean fidgeted anxiously with the handkerchief in her pocket as they strolled by the boating lake. The late afternoon sunlight shimmered on the water as children shouted and laughed darting happily in and out along the water's edge. Both were lost in thought as they walked watching the children squeal with delight; the air was thick with sadness at the forthcoming separation, but Jean was unprepared for Ken's next words.

Ken stopped suddenly on the dusty path; turning to grasp Jean by the shoulders pulling her round to face him; he held her gaze for what seemed like eternity before he spoke; his deep emerald, blue eyes searching her face.

"Jean" his voice low and husky; his breath warm on her face; his eyes filled with apprehension and urgency

"You know by now how I feel about you don't you? How I have always felt about you"

Jean held her breath not wanting to hear what she knew was about to be spoken.

"There could never be anyone else like you Jean; you bring sunshine to the cloudiest day" but, Jean was thinking I can hear but, please don't say it! "But you know that this is our most dangerous posting yet? No matter how much I love you my little Jeanie. it would be wrong of me to expect you to wait for me. You know I may not make it back; have fun Jean; live your life and do what makes you happy. With those words he drew her close to him; cupping his hands behind her head; his fingers entwined in her silky hair.

Jean could feel his warm muscular chest through her blouse and her heart seemed to thud so fast beneath her ribs that she was sure he could feel it too; her skin prickled hotly with eager anticipation. and then he kissed her; with such passion and intensity Jean never wanted it to end; his mouth so soft and warm against hers; his breath gently caressing her cheek. Yes, he had kissed her before but never like this; Jean felt as if she was floating on gossamer clouds but as their lips parted; Jean breathless and flushed; he pulled back sharply.

"Goodbye Jean; I will never forget you" he practically whispered and before Jean had chance to open her mouth to protest, he whipped around and hurried away from her. Stunned Jean had made her way home, tears rolling down her cheeks; not caring if anyone saw her for her heart was truly broken.

Now many months had passed without so much as a letter from him; but she had kept in touch with his mum Auntie Vi as her and Jack had called her since they were kids, so she knew that he was okay. Jean knew that the battalion that both boys belonged to were due home anytime. She allowed herself to daydream; what if they are back already maybe he will be there tonight? Her stomach flip flopped at the thought of him! Yes, she had many admirers especially the American boys, but Jean had stayed true; no one could hold a flame to him; she knew what her heart wanted.

Ah here is the bus at last; and here come Dotty huffing and puffing as she comes rushing around the corner; holding onto her skirt as the wind whips around her threatening to show off tomorrow's washing. Her apple blossom is barely restrained beneath her low-cut tight blouse, bouncing, and jiggling as she tries to run which was difficult in her new red stiletto shoes. Her wild blonde spring like curls; as usual untamed; blowing wildly around her round face. Poor Dotty thought Jean; her vivacious friend; always a little on the chubby side; no matter how hard she tried she always seemed to look a bit like an unmade bed. But that didn't stop her where the boys were concerned; they loved her generous frame; her voluptuous curves and not to forget her buxom assets that always seemed to be trying to spill out of her clothes; no, the guys always made a beeline for Dotty.

"Come on Dot" Jean hollers encouraging her friend; as they jump on the bus just in time; giggling they take their seats.

"Have you heard the news, Jeanie?" Dotty asks excitedly. Jean looks at her expectantly.

"They are back Jean; the boys are back!" Mum just came in she said she saw your Jack on his way home" "isn't that great" she jabs Jean in the ribs with her elbow; "you know what this means don't you?" Jean stares at her blankly; "your Ken will be home by now too; maybe he will be at the dance tonight!" her eyes gleam with merriment as she waits for Jeans response.

"He is not my Ken" exclaims Jean "he made that quite clear when he left" Jean fiddles with the hem of her dress; not looking her friend in the eye and trying not to rub her clammy palms on the beautiful material.

"But he is back Jeanie babe; I'm sure he didn't mean what he said, I am sure he will want you back" "you know you two were always meant to be together!" Jean feels her stomach roll and lurch nervously; the ham salad she ate for tea threatening to make a reappearance.

"Anyway" sniffed Jean "maybe I don't want him back; there are plenty more fish in the sea"

Her friend smiled kindly at her. "He told me not to wait for him Dot; that meant he wasn't saving himself for me" she shifts in her seat and turns quickly to look out of the window, wiping away the solitary tear that rolled down her cheek before Dotty noticed.

"Yes, okay Hun; she pats her friend's arm sympathetically; "but let's just wait and see, eh? The bus lurches to a halt by the old bombed out church as the girl's sway down the aisle and hop off onto the busy road. Town is busy; lots of activity and a sense of hope fills the air. People seem happy; maybe war will soon be over, thinks Jean; life must get better then surely; maybe back to normal again, although what is normal? Jean ponders as the girl's arm in arm, make their way round the corner to the dance hall.

As they pass by once beautiful church Jean is filled with gloom; its stunning stained-glass windows gone; walls crushed and abandoned, nothing but rubble left; it's so, so sad. Mum and dad were married here and Jack and Jean both christened in the lovely parish church; now sadly in ruins; poor mum can't bear to come into town anymore.

Butterflies in Jean's tummy are doing the rumba again as Dotty pushes open the door to the dance hall ahead of her. As the door thuds close behind them, they are immediately enveloped in the heat of the stuffy crowded room; the rhythmic sound of the band filling the air, the smell of cigarette smoke cloying as a cloud seems to hover over the crowd, Jean hates the stink of cigarettes but so many seem to smoke these days even her own father ,yuck she thinks I don't want to dance with anyone who smells of stinky fags!

The dance floor is already full as the lads in uniform, especially American, fill the large

square glossy polished floor, pretty girls resplendent in their best dancing skirts and dresses hanging on to each of them, smiling, laughing, twisting, and twirling to the lively music.

The girls sit down at one of the only free tables around the dance floor, Dotty chuckles as the cheap wooden chair groans under her padded frame then squeaks as she shuffles it closer to Jean's so they can assess the talent together. Jean absent-mindedly picks at the peeling Formica around the edge of the small, tatty table as the girls scan the crowd for familiar faces. Jean's heart soars as she spots a small group of lads in British uniform on the opposite side of the room, but it sinks just as quickly when she can't see him. Dotty is prodding her in the arm, wildly, urgently.

"Ow Dotty! Give over I can see them, but he's not there" Jean's mood is clouding over fast as she is beginning to regret coming out tonight. What was I thinking, even if he is home, he is hardly going to come dancing tonight is he? And if Dotty's mum is correct maybe she should go home and see Jack?

"There"! Dotty is practically shouting now! "He is over at the bar with his cousin Sam" Jean swivels in her chair for a better look, scanning the mass of uniformed bodies jostling at the bar trying to get served. Jean's breath catches in her throat as she spots him, every hair on her scalp stands to attention, every skin cell tingled as she feels a warm rush of blood to her face.

"Oh Dotty" she exclaimed "he's here! At last, "oh what am I to do, keep watching" she couldn't look any longer, "tell me if he is coming over" Jean couldn't contain herself, she couldn't ever recall feeling like this before. And then he turned, and their eyes locked across the swaying dancers. Everything seemed to come to a standstill in that moment, Jean could barely breath as his eyes held her hostage in their gaze. No longer able to stand the tension Jean stood and started to advance across the floor. She stops about 6 feet away, he is standing right in front of her smiling, when suddenly he is spun round by a tall willowy blonde who has grasped him by the wrist.

"Come on Kenny", Jean didn't recognize the gorgeous girl now holding his attention, "dance with me".

Jean stopped dead in her tracks not waiting to see his reaction, she ran from the room as fast as her legs would carry her, out past the kissing couples by the toilets, out of the main doors, into the crisp evening air. She paused gulping for air, the world spinning around her. "How stupid am I" she sobbed to herself, tears now cursing down her face, her heart ached, "why would I even think he would still be interested in Me!" Regaining her

composure, she decides there is nothing else to do but make her way home, when she feels a warm hand upon her shoulder.

"Jeanie wait!" Ken grasped both of her shoulders as he spun her around to face him. She could feel the warmth of his hands through the thin fabric of her dress, the blood cursing through her veins and pounding in her ears as she brushed the tears from her cheeks.

"Oh, babe why are you running away, I've waited so long for this moment" he pulled her closer now, so close she could feel his soft breath on her face.

"I thought you were never coming back" Jean looked down at her shoes, not daring to look him in the eye,

"I, that girl, I didn't think you would want me anymore?" emotion now overwhelming her, Jean's knees start to buckle as she leans into him.

"That girl, Jean, is no one, it's you I want, it's only ever been you, my beautiful Jeanie"

Jean gathers herself feeling stronger, wraps her arms around his waist, confidence growing he leans down and presses his lips against hers, kissing her with such urgency, the taste of his lips exquisite upon hers.

He releases her gently, removing her hands from around his waist, and bends one knee to kneel on the path before her. Oh, my Jean clasps her hand to her mouth, realizing now what he is saying she can't stop the corners of her mouth curling up into the widest smile.

"Be mine forever Jeanie" Ken holds out his hand to take hers, "let's never be apart again?"

Just as she is about to reply, the dance hall doors burst open and masses of bodies are spilling out, shouting, laughing, singing with obvious delight.

"It's over!" a young man in a grey uniform is shouting, "The Nazi's have surrendered! War is over"

The air is filled with delirious people dancing around them. Mary pushes the tea trolley into the lounge of Sunny Vally retirement home, dozens of the residents slumped in wing backed chairs all around the room, some sleeping, some reading or knitting and some just staring into space, it's a sad end to life thinks Mary as she sets the cups and saucers out on her trolley.

"Wake up Jean, she approaches one of her favourite ladies, shaking her shoulder slightly,

"Come on me dear, it's time for a cuppa, you know you enjoy a good brew."

Jean gasps slightly startled awake from her dream," yes, yes, Ken of course I will marry you!"

She blinks in the bright afternoon light taking in Mary's form before her.

"No, no, no yells Jean, desperately ripped from her lovely memories. She closes her eyes, and a soft gurgle emits from her throat, I'm coming home Ken, we will be together once again, forever.

Frederick Peverill

Madeleine sighs as she locks the door to her family home for the final time. She places the key inside her handbag, picks up the pet carrier, and the plastic bag containing an old family photo album which she had previously placed on the doorstep.

"Come on Freddie," she says, "Let's go and get you settled into your new home."

Fred looks at her thinking to himself, here we go again. Fred is a Birman pedigree cat; he is a beautiful specimen despite his age. He has a long silky cream coloured coat, a broad dark brown face, tail, and ears that are as wide as they are tall. His eyes are a beautiful shade of blue. His paws however are snow white; he looks as though he has four white socks upon them. He is a very special cat indeed. Madeleine is yet to discover that he can talk as well as any human being and is incredibly old, in fact well over one hundred years all told. He has many a tale to tell her once she realises just what she has adopted.

Over recent weeks Madeleine has almost lived at the family home, she has been decluttering the large, detached house in which she was born. Both her parents have now passed away, gone to their final resting place. Her father was first to go, it was a blessing really. He had developed Alzheimer's disease and needed twenty-four-hour care towards the end. Her mother, Dorothy, had remained stoic throughout, insisting her father stayed at home until the end. Madeleine recalls how gaunt and tired her mother had looked in those final days. She knew her mother wouldn't last long after her father's death and she had been right. Within six months Dorothy was no more. Madeleine was sad but also relieved at the same time. She would now sell the house and do as she had promised to take care of Fred as long as he lived. She suddenly thinks back, Fred has always been around for as long as she can remember. He has been living at the house for at least forty years that she knows of. Good gracious she thinks, he really must be incredibly old poor thing. I'm going to care for him and spoil him in just the way he deserves.

Upon arrival at her flat, she puts the photo album on the coffee table, rescues Fred from the carrier and says,

"Right Fred, do you want something to eat and drink. I'll put some food over here and a saucer of milk for you."

She busies herself as she speaks, at the same time, she makes a cup of tea and takes a couple of chocolate biscuits from the tin. Fred tucks into his food, laps up his milk and makes his way into the sitting room. Madeleine follows suit, tea in one hand, biscuits in the other. She sits down gratefully and picks up the photo album as she does so. Fred jumps up onto her knee and makes himself comfortable.

The photos have all been carefully fastened into the album, each has a date written underneath them, although there are no names or indication of who these people are. She doesn't recognise anyone other than her mum, dad, and grandma, but she thinks that's generally the way with old photos, without realising she is speaking out loud.

"It's a shame really isn't it – all these forgotten faces, no-one left to tell us who they might be or what lives they have led."

Fred suddenly looks up towards her, his dark blue eyes piercing into hers. To her surprise, Fred suddenly speaks to her in a distinctly French accent.

"I know who these people are, if you would like me to tell you."

Madeleine looks down at the cat in amazement, she grimaces and says out loud, "I've been doing too much, I must have, I've just heard Fred talk to me, that cannot be right, or can it? I better watch my step, or they will be carting me away." She pulls Fred towards her and strokes his silky coat as she does so. Fred stares up at her again,

"Ma Cherie, you are not crazy, I can talk, I just don't make a habit of it that's all. Allez! show me the first photo and I will explain it to you."

Madeleine opens the album. The photo on display is a family group dated 1890. She peers closely at the photo and realises Fred is sitting in there alongside these unfamiliar people. She turns towards him with a quizzical expression on her face.

"Mais Oui" Fred says "I remember it well, the photo is of Maman, Papa, Grand'Mere, and Grand Pere and my very first owner, Lucette. As you can see, she is holding me on her knee – not too carefully I can tell you. She was holding me by the neck tightly, so she didn't drop me. I nearly choked to death in the process. I remember getting quite a hard smack on the derriere by the photographer for patting and plucking the tassels on the curtain he used as the backdrop to the photo. I didn't really like him very much."

Fred looks around the flat with disdain.

"I started my life with this family, they had a beautiful home in Paris. Papa had just returned home from Myanmar. I was born there but was given to Papa by a Buddhist monk because he had been so taken with my markings. I don't blame him actually; I was an exceptionally fine specimen of my breed way back then."

Fred stands, stretches, and circles around Madeleine's lap and starts preening himself.

"Oh, and just for the record," he says lifting his nose skywards, "I want you to know I am an Aristocrat and have extremely high standards which you will have to live up to. My proper name is Frederic Peverell, although everyone has always called me Fred for short, I don't really mind that actually. Lucette and I spent many happy hours playing together. I felt a little put out when she dressed me in her doll's clothes but quite enjoyed our trips down the garden being pushed in her doll's pram. I used to pretend I was the king in my golden coach. We also played with coloured glass marbles, which was fun, but we usually ended up getting in trouble some way or another.

Maddie turns the page. The next photo is of a rosy buxom lady wearing a white stiff apron and cap, there sat in pride of place on a small table at the side of her is Fred, the date underneath the photo is 1902. Fred looks at it for several minutes.

"Ah Mon Dieu!" this is a sad moment for me, my best friend and playmate had recently passed away. She had contracted Typhus and no matter how hard everyone tried to save her they couldn't do it. It was so quiet after she had gone, Maman and Papa decided to go away on a long trip across Europe to try and get over her loss. Lucette had been the light in everyone's life in our Parisian home, she was missed dreadfully. Cook had agreed to take care of me while they were away. I must admit she did care for me very well, but Maman and Papa never returned, losing Lucette proved too much for them, Cook eventually got a new post when the family home was sold. She did take me with her, but her new employers would not allow her to keep me, and so she begged the local farrier to take me in.

The next photo is dated 1903 and is of a large man, strongly built stood next to his anvil leaning on his large hammer. He has a large beaming smile across his face. Fred is sat looking at him sitting proudly on the window ledge situated above his left shoulder. He looks long and hard at the photo and eventually speaks,

"Voila! That is Francois, the local farrier, he was a truly kind man, he really loved the horses and any other waif or stray that crossed his path. It was at this point my life began to change. I was no longer cossetted, brushed, or fed sweetmeats, I had to some degree fend for myself. I was expected to keep the rats and mice population down in exchange for my keep. I was useless at first but gradually got the hang of it."

Fred looks aloofly at Madeleine,

"Well one has to do what is necessary to survive don't you agree? we all need to do that."

Madeleine nods in agreement as Fred continues,

"Life was OK, but once again my luck ran out. In 1916 Francois's business had almost dried up, every available horse for miles around had been commandeered to help soldiers on the front line, defending our wonderful country from the ravages of the Germans. Eventually Francois was called up to fight in the war and sadly never returned. He was killed in action, I really missed him. His brother Jacques took me in after that, so my life continued much the same as before."

The next photo is dated 1917, Jacques is sitting on a chair adjacent to a hospital bed, Fred is sat next to him on the bed looking very superior. Fred continues to explain,

"Jacque's friend took this photo. They both worked together in an army medical hospital taking care of the sick and wounded as they returned from the front."

While Fred talks on, Madeleine has been calculating Fred's age and suddenly interrupts him,

"Do you realise Freddie you were twenty-six years old when you went to live with Jacques, and to be honest you don't look more than one year older even now. Why is this do you think?"

Fred sits quietly purring,

"Bien! Have you not realised yet, I am a very special cat? As you know cats have nine lives and I am determined to enjoy every one of them.

"Do you know I was given a new title when we lived at the hospital unit. I became known as the hospital cat, rat catcher and saver of souls. I was often called upon to sit and nuzzle up to soldiers, especially those affected by shell shock. They seem to quieten when I lay down beside them. They used to stroke and brush me and tell me all their problems. I was well fed, probably better than everyone else actually, because all the soldiers shared their meagre rations with me. I must admit with my dynamic personality everyone loved me.

The next photo is dated 1918 and is of a frail young man, dressed in civilian clothes holding Fred under his arm, a suitcase standing at his feet.

As Madeleine looks at the photo, she points to it saying,

"I know who this man is, he was my grandma's brother, his name was Peter, I believe he suffered greatly during the war. He was completely traumatised by all the death and destruction he had seen during his stay in France and was barely holding himself together when he returned home. So sad really." she sighs at the thought of it all.

Fred is quiet for a few minutes before continuing his tale.

"It took us quite a while to make our way up to Peter's Lancashire home, his parents were thrilled to be able to welcome him back and were more than happy to adopt me as well. I think they were actually grateful to me for being Peter's constant companion. He said nothing to anyone in the family, he just didn't want to talk, but would whisper things to me when he thought no-one was listening. The family home was warm and comfortable, but Mon Dieu the weather in this Blighty is not good. It is always dreary, cold, and wet and not compatible with my silky coat, it became a permanent chore licking and grooming myself in order to maintain my dignity. Over the years though I have learned to accept it, but oh how I miss my beloved France.

After Peter's return home, life went on fairly quietly. In 1925, Dorothy your mother, was born and brought renewed joy to everyone in the home. Peter and I used to snuggle up close to your mum and each other. I remember well, your grandparents were always ready with their camera to get snapshots of us all at every opportunity. See look there is one they took soon after Dorothy was born." Peter has Fred sat on his knee, and the proud parents sit beside him with the newborn baby in their arms.

"As your mum grew up, I seemed to start experiencing the same life as I had in Paris with Lucette. We became firm friends and played the same games. The dratted doll's clothes were back on the scene, rides in the perambulator too. We also played marbles, I loved showing off my extremely adept footwork skills and acrobatic moves to everyone. Poor Peter didn't live very long, he lost more and more weight until eventually he lost his strength and will to carry on. Your mum promised him that she would love and care for me as he had done, and she did.

In 1948 your mum was married and started a new life, they took me with them of course and we all went to live in the big house which we have just left behind. In 1950 you, Madeleine, were born. As you can see the last photo in the album is of us all, me sitting on maman's lap, and you being proudly held in your papa's arms."

Fred jumps down from Madeleine's knee and looks up at her and says,

"Thirsty work all this story telling, can I have some more milk do you think?"

Madeleine picks up her empty teacup and follows Fred back into the kitchen. She still is a little unsure what has been happening this afternoon and decides to ask Fred how he has managed to live so long.

"Fred why exactly have you been able to live such a long life, do you know?"

Fred turns round stares at her and says,

"I'm not too sure, but I do know when I lived in Myanmar, I was a special cat, because my maman told me. She said I would live to be one hundred years old and that I must enjoy every moment of it. Make the most of it she said and live a happy life. I think I have managed to do that, and I am grateful to have lived such a long, and varied life and now in my twilight years hope to carry on doing the same until I am called to cross the rainbow bridge."

"Well Fred I will do my best to see you do that." Madeleine strokes him gently as she speaks.

After several months, Madeleine is happy, her parents' house has been sold and the money has been deposited into her bank account. She will be able to move now to her permanent home. She looks over to Fred who is stretched out along the back of the sofa basking in the afternoon sunlight.

"Guess what Freddie, you and I are going on another adventure. I am sure you will be very pleased to know, we are going to live in Marseilles, and you will be able to see out your days living and sleeping in the warm sunshine of your beloved France. Shall we take a photo before we start the next chapter of our life."

Fred rolls over, stretches, and jumps down from the sofa, and runs over to Madeleine, he rubs his head on her leg and merely says,

"Merci, I cannot wait to go home."

Festival Child

I'm emotionally exhausted as I sit here nursing a cup of coffee, remembering the fateful night that baby Willow first came into our lives.

After thirty-eight years in the NHS and surviving working frontline in the covid pandemic, I re-evaluated my priorities and retired from the hustle and bustle of my nursing post in a busy Accident and Emergency unit.

I wasn't quite ready for sitting and slippers and was looking for adventure and fun.
Now it was time for me and my already retired husband Jim to do something for us and enjoy our newfound freedom. I was proud to be a sixties child and used to enjoy going to concerts and music gigs in my youth. I wrote a bucket list and decided I would like to go to Glastonbury, but Jim wasn't keen!
I was a bit disappointed that he didn't want to go,

but he promised we would go on holiday together later in the year. Somewhere we would both enjoy.

Jim was so relieved when my good friend Donna, the original hippy chick and earth mother with pink streaks in her hair and colourful clothes, invited me to apply to be a steward with her, at Glastonbury festival 2023, and he could stay home tending his allotment.

Donna had been a steward at the festival in 2022, but I had been working that year and was unable to go with her on that occasion. I couldn't wait to go this year, after hearing her reminisce about her experiences. We had to have first aid training and an up-to-date child protection certificate and get there the day before the event at Worthy farm in Somerset, to get used to the area and meet our other steward team members. With my history as an A and E nurse, I passed the application process with ease. We were going to stay in Donna's vintage camper van and arrived as expected after suffering a minor delay due to a punctured tyre. The area was vast and the pyramid stage daunting. I couldn't wait to see the bands performing on that stage. The food stalls were already set up. We weren't going to go hungry, that was for sure and to my amazement, five hundred mobile toilets were delivered and were placed at intervals around the fields.

People wanting a good spot near the stage had

already started to arrive and were setting up their tents in the allocated field.
The VIP/artist's area was cordoned off and final checks were made.

The first day of the festival arrived and Michael the organiser, who has been running Glastonbury festival on his land, since 1970, gave us stewards a very inspirational speech about enjoying the experience and keeping people safe, then handed us over to chief steward Geoff.

Geoff was a good friend of Michael's and had a large mobile home on the fields near to the area reserved for the artists trailers. I was appreciative of the fact that he had a good supply of emergency equipment, torches, blankets, waterproof clothing, and bottled water. This obviously wasn't his first rodeo and he made me feel safe, especially when he said his golden rule was always, "Call for back up."
We coordinated our phone numbers with Geoff and the other stewards and were issued with radios, a first aid kit, a fluorescent overcoat, and a torch each.

I had seen Glastonbury on the TV before, but being there was a whole new experience. The crowds were massive, people as far as the eye could see, enjoying the music and dancing, having the time of their lives.

The atmosphere was electric and addictive. I walked miles in my role as a steward and enjoyed every minute of it. It was good to be needed and I used my trusty pocket first aid kit on a couple of occasions.
I was amazed that for such a large crowd, everything was harmonious, and I never saw any falling out. No pushing or jostling as we'd experienced at other rock concerts in the past. People were just looking out for each other and enjoying the festival.

The food stalls did a roaring trade and the smell of cooked onions, bacon and sickly-sweet popcorn hung in the air. The music was amazing, and the artists gave their all. An unusual highlight of the event was that two baby owls were rescued from under the pyramid stage after their parents were disturbed by the music, when rock band Guns and Roses performed! They baby owls were named Axl and Slash after band members and were taken by a wildlife sanctuary. Jim would have loved that. His favourite band is Guns and Roses.

It was the last night of Glastonbury festival, and the crowds were bigger than ever. One hundred and seventy thousand strong, they waited for Elton to headline this year's event, part of his Farewell Yellow Brick Road tour.
That man put his heart and soul into his performance The crowds were mesmerised as he

rocked out hit after hit, splendidly enrobed in a gold suit and his trademark glasses.
He introduced his guests with respect giving them a chance to shine and there wasn't a dry eye, when he gave an emotive tribute to his friend George Michael on what would have been his 60th birthday and thanked the crowds and his fans worldwide for their support.
As the last bars of his final song, Rocket Man came to an end, the sky erupted with the most spectacular firework display, filling the air with pops of colour and crackling light.
The crowd went wild, and applause was stupendous as the noise rang around the festival site. It had been a momentous performance, one never to be forgotten.

Elton was reluctant to leave, but eventually took his final bow and was raised up from the stage, through an open door and whisked away by his helicopter to take him home to his family. I bet he was exhausted as I was!

The massive crowds began to disperse, some going back to their tents, others rushing to their cars and joining the gridlock, trying to get away from the fields. Donna and I were staying to help with the clean-up operation.
My inner eco warrior was horrified at the amount of rubbish left behind. Plastic cups and polystyrene food trays were strewn everywhere,

and tents just left behind by the revellers, but I had been reassured that it would all soon be cleaned up, and the abandoned tents and bedding would be going to local homeless shelters.

In a few days, the fields would be back to normal, and people would already be speculating as to which artists would perform next year.
I knew that I would be coming back but I doubted anything could top the performance I had just witnessed from Elton. I thought, I might even persuade Jim to come next year.

I stood, soaking up the atmosphere, alone with my thoughts, despite the hum of thousands of people around me going about their business. I didn't want the night to end and wandered slowly round the field. The air was choked with smoke from the fireworks and as the crowds dispersed the vast litter problem became more evident.
Clean up didn't start until tomorrow, so I meandered slowly back to find Donna.

I had wandered to the edge of the field as it wasn't quite as muddy. The noise from the roaring crowds had subsided a little and it was a clear, starry night. As I gazed at the stars, I heard a baby crying and wondered what ever would possess anyone to bring a baby to a music festival. There it was again, a thin feeble cry and suddenly, my senses were alert! I just knew that something wasn't right, and I had to find where that cry was coming from. I walked in the direction; I thought the cry had come from and shouted out to the mother of the baby to ask if she was, ok? There was no response, so I started to search the abandoned tents. As I entered the third tent, and shone my torch, I was shocked that there were no adults about. I had expected to see the baby's mother or at least a responsible adult. A whimpering little cry came from the bed area. There was blood on the sleeping bag and a towel, and I held my breath as I uncovered a tiny newborn baby girl, still attached to her placenta, and wrapped in the sleeping bag. There was a note scribbled on a paper donut bag that said.

"Please look after Willow. I can't care for her."

My heart was breaking when I read the message, and I couldn't help feeling sad. I wondered if the woman who had recently given birth had been alone and how desperate she must have felt. Why had she had her baby here? Why didn't she go to the maternity hospital? No-one would have heard her painful cries with the noise from loud music, excited crowds, and those fireworks. My A and E background kicked in and I immediately felt the cord. It had stopped pulsating. I had heard of lots of deliveries where the placenta remained attached to the baby and I wasn't about to do any heroics in the middle of a muddy field and try to separate the baby's cord, even though I did have a small pair of scissors in my first aid kit.

I knew that she needed to be kept warm, so I quickly discarded my tee shirt and wiped her down and tucked her inside my sweatshirt next to my skin. I wrapped the placenta in a discarded carrier bag and put into in my sweatshirt pocket to keep it safe.
She stopped crying as I cuddled her, and Geoff's mantra rang in my head,

"Always call for backup."

I fished my mobile out of my coat and rang his number but there was a no signal, Typical! I abandoned the mobile and thank goodness, was able to use the back-up radio to get Geoff's attention. I put out the call and was relieved to hear Geoff's voice.

"Hi, Geoff here is there a problem? please give me your location"

I half expected Willow's mum to reappear any minute and ask what I was doing with her baby, but the harsh reality that Willow had been abandoned was all too clear.

 Geoff and another steward arrived in a golf buggy approx. fifteen minutes later. It was the longest fifteen minutes of my life, but I shall forever treasure the memory, of my surreal experience where there was just me and Willow, snuggled together in the tent by torch light.

Whilst he expressed his surprise and said this had never happened before, Geoff was the ultimate professional and in no time at all had called the police and local maternity unit, assigned the other steward to tape off the area around the tent and guard it until the police arrives and escorted me back to his warm mobile home.

Geoff was incredibly well prepared for every eventuality, from his store of provisions, he produced a bottle of baby milk, a blanket and a clean tee shirt and sweatshirt for me. Willow was jittery and I guessed it was because she needed food and was relieved when she took a bottle hungrily and then fell asleep.

A policeman arrived and asked a few questions before organising a search for the baby's mother and an ambulance transferred me and baby to the local maternity unit, where we were met by Judith, a kindly senior midwife in her crisp, navy uniform.

Judith thoroughly checked baby over with her experienced eye and swiftly clamped and cut the cord and removed the placenta to a specimen pot. She called for a paediatrician, and both agreed that baby looked around term gestation but a bit small and thankfully in good condition thanks to the care she had already received.

Willow would need to stay in hospital for observations and to see if Mum could be found and of course social services would be called in. I felt very protective towards my little foundling and asked if I could stay in touch?

 I told the staff that my daughter Evangeline and husband Chris were emergency foster carers. They had been unable to conceive a child of their own and after years of invasive tests and heartbreaking failed IVF attempts. They eventually gave up trying and instead trained to be emergency/short term foster parents.

 Judith settled Willow in a cot and made me a much-needed cup of tea, whilst she rang matron at home to update her on the situation and ask permission for me to visit.
Matron gave permission for me to visit the next day and advised Judith to give my daughter's details to the social worker.
Reluctantly, once Willow was transferred to the maternity ward, I got a taxi back to the festival ground and left her in the very capable hands of Judith and her team.

Donna was waiting anxiously for me to return. The adrenaline flowed and we couldn't sleep, so we stayed up all night chatting in her van, wrapped in comfortable blankets, sipping hot chocolate, and munching our way through a tin of shortbread biscuits.

The hospital and police issued a joint statement and encouraged Mum to come forward in case she needed medical help and I rand Jim and Evangeline to share my news.
Jim wasn't surprised as he often said that excitement and drama followed me everywhere. Evangeline was proud and excited. She contacted the maternity unit and offered to take Willow into foster care, when she was fit to leave hospital, if her Mum wasn't found.

The next morning, Donna and I helped to dismantle tents and pack sleeping bags to go to the local homeless shelters. My priority for the afternoon was to visit my little foundling, Willow. She was being thoroughly loved and cared for by the maternity staff and I was introduced to Danni her social worker. I told Danni about my daughter and her husband wanting to be her emergency foster parents and she promised to let the judge know. In the absence of her parents, all decisions would have to be made, in Willow's best interests, when they went to family court. It was ideal as they would want Willow to go to foster parents in a different area from where she had been found.

Despite plenty of news coverage where the local paper had christened little Willow "Festival child" and the police carried out a door-to-door search, Willow's Mother wasn't found. It was like she had melted into the crowds.

Lots of people came forward and offered to care for Willow, but to our delight the judged approved Evangeline and Chris as her new foster parents.

After a few weeks, Evangeline and Chris decided that they would like to adopt Willow and Danni was incredibly supportive helping them with their adoption application.

Eight months have now passed since that fateful day when I found Willow and after many rigorous checks, a miracle has occurred.
The judge, after considering, the note that was found and again, Willow's best interests, approved Evangeline, and Chris to become adoptive parents. Today we received the wonderful news and had a celebration tea this afternoon.

Surprisingly, Danni also dropped by to see us. She was beside herself, excitedly sharing, that she had been contacted by some of the rock stars who performed at Glastonbury. They had been following Willow's story in the news.
Although they wish to remain anonymous, Danni said that they have generously put money into a trust fund for when she is twenty-one. What a lucky little girl she is.
I can't help wondering where her birth Mum is. I

wish I could speak to her.

She was so selfless to give Willow up for a better life and I pray that wherever she is, she is ok and has seen the news footage and knows that her precious little festival child is safe and well.

The Prom

Aimee sat on her bed cross legged with her back supported by the headboard and pillows and had a cold drink and a large family sized bag of crisps on the bedside table. Through her headphones was playing the current popular music by a group she thought were the best band ever, which her parents described nothing but a loud din with no structure or beat. Aimee totally disagreed and daydreamed what it would be like to be one of the bands girlfriends. Failing that she would jump at the chance of Roman Kemp, the radio one DJ.

Aimee was horrified when she said this to her sister one lunch time her mum had said how at her age, she would have liked to go out with his dad Martin kemp. What made it worse was her dad muttered he thought Shirlee, Roman's mum was quite a looker when she was younger. Both girls pretended to put their fingers down their throat to imitate being sick.

Aimee felt more than a little lost now all her revising had ended. She had sat doing a couple of games on her iPad, the last game she had been stuck on level 211 for what seemed an age. She had no more lives to play now for another half an hour which was quite annoying for her

"Hi, Aims what you are doing?" asked Kate, Aimee's sister "oh don't tell me your seeing what Jade is up to again on Facebook and Instagram."

"NO, I am not" she replied angrily even though she was and annoyed that Kate was right. Secretly she hoped and prayed that one day she could be as popular as Jade.

To Aimee, Jade had everything, a good figure, shiny waist length blonde hair, perfect teeth, lovely complexion and had every boy in school fawning over her.

The main conversation on face book currently was the upcoming end of school Prom. So exciting booking hair up and nail appointments.

The boys were just as excited on Facebook discussing suits, whether to have a bow tie or long tie. Button down collars, long sleeved shirts or short.

Trying on long evening dresses that belonged in a Disney film, matching handbag, and shoes. Booking leg and underarm waxing and not forgetting the spray tans.

Aimee and her school friends wanted to arrive at the venue in a stretched black limo, unfortunately after booking the limousine the company had informed Aimee's mum that they had double booked and they in their words could not apologise enough. After ringing everywhere in the area Aimee's mum had been told the same thing repeatedly that all the limos in the area had been booked for months before. Mum told Aimee who had then to tell her friends who were all totally Gutted every one-off them. Aimee's mum had said she, jokingly that she would drop off Aimee and a friend at the venue on her way to work. To which Aimee was horrified at the thoughts of her mum pulling in front of Kilhey Court the schools chosen venue in her old ford fiesta.

Of course, Jade had booked a limo and was playing games with the girls to see who she would let in her limo.

Jade asked Aimee if she would like to travel in her Limo, overjoyed Aimee said she would be thrilled to which Jade said later in the week that unfortunately there was no room for her.

Aimee sobbed for what seemed forever.

"Jade is on the train going to Manchester to get her prom dress" said Aimee (scrolling through social media) to Kate "I bet she has the best dress at the prom not like me with a second hand one."

"Your dress is gorgeous, and you are lucky to have it. No one around here will have seen it or the pictures of Lucy last year at her prom so cut it out and stop whining will you."

"And for your information when I left the station earlier Jade, and her mum were on the Southport platform so she must have been going to see her Nan."

Various notifications came up from friends who had been having a practice hair up at the hairdressers. Friends posting back that the hair styles were amazing, appointments booked for the day of the prom. A multitude of pictures with nails every colour imaginable, false nail like talons with comments like "Not sure how I am going to wipe my bum" followed by a succession of laughing emojis.

"Jade has tried on loads of dresses; her mum apparently has said that the price is irrelevant and that she can pick which ever she wants." Said Aimee heavily. "Everyone is saying how lucky she is."

"No limit on the price, she is having you on, she is leading you all on by the nose and you are all following her "scoffed Kate "telling you she was getting the Southport train to Ormskirk to see her Nan. Manchester is in the opposite direction by the way."

Kate got on Aimee's nerves sometimes especially when Jade was the subject on face book.

. "Jade is telling you all a pack of lies and you are all taken in with her."

"How do you know she is telling lies smarty pants "

"I can always tell she is lying because Her lips move" sniggered Kate.

"Sod off Kate" said Aimee pulling a disgruntled face at her.

Aimee got up from the bed her legs like jelly from being crossed leg for so long and went downstairs to see what her mum was cooking for their evening meal.

"You girls will have to see to yourselves tonight as your dad and I are going out with your dad's work mate and his new wife." said mum getting a pizza out of the freezer "We are going to that new restaurant on Wigan Lane it's got some good reviews and apparently the wine is reasonable. We are really looking forward to meeting the new Mrs."

"Oh, you mean we have to share a crust of stale bread why you two stuff your faces with an Italian meal, great." said Aimee.

"There is enough food in the fridge, cupboards and freezer to keep you going for days." replied the mum placing the pizza on the work surface.

"We will be skin and bone when you get back, Aimee ring ChildLine now tell them we are children left to our own devices while these two go out to eat and do not spare a thought for us. Come sister we will die in each other's arms" said Kate being all dramatic.

"I seem to remember there is Kebab meat and them bread pocket things in the freezer, also frozen chips we can have those, watch a film on Netflix and drink some of mums cider" said Aimee cheekily "when we have eaten and drunk up then we can ring ChildLine because we don't want Ester coming in and sharing a kebab and nicking our chips.

Mum put the pizza back into the fridge shaking her head in disbelief.

Laughter filled the kitchen and then Aimee's phone pinged which meant there was a new notification on Facebook...

"What has Jade got now, is she travelling to kilhey court in her own private helicopter" said Kate nudging her mum to get her attention.

"Kate stop winding Aimee up, and Aimee take everything Jade is saying with a pinch of salt, "said mum.

"Jade has got the most exquisite shoes and handbag to match they are gorgeous aren't they" said Aimee showing the family the Facebook picture of the glistening shoes and matching clutch bag and sending out a big sigh of Dispur.

"I seem to have seen that picture before," said Kate thoughtfully.

"Oh yes it does seem familiar," said mum.

"Maybe Jade's mum has put it on Facebook" said Aimee clearly feeling a little hard done to

"I know I have seen that picture before somewhere recently." Said Kate still looking at the picture and trying to remember where she had seen it recently.

"No, you haven't liar" screeched Aimee "you so get on my nerves."

"She'll break her neck in them, the heels are a good four inch" said Dad hovering over his three girls as he liked to relate to them proudly.

.

Further pictures came upon Jade's Facebook page showing very fashionable and expensive hair salons, beauty parlours where Jade had been booked into.

Then came a spa day for Jade arranged by her grandmother.

"SPA Day!" laughed her dad when Aimee told him the following morning "the only Spar old Ma Higgins knows is at the end of the street where she lived before going into the nursing home. You are becoming obsessed by Jade, does it matter if she is escorted to Kilhey court by King Charles, at the end of the day you are all going to have a good time, you are all on the same pathway to wonderful careers.

Do not let the likes of Jade spoil your evening, Jade's dad was always a blagger, he could talk his way into any job until he was found out he had not got the foggiest how to do the job."

The leavers prom was becoming closer, and the excitement was growing around the school leavers, their friends, and relations.

"Hello Helen" said Mum getting up from the table where the family had just finished their evening meal "do you want a brew?"

"Oh no I have brought this" said Helen holding a bottle of fizz up in the air.

"I think we are in for a little celebration."

"Bloody beltin have we won the lottery, and you are sharing it with your favourite brother-in-law." Said dad smiling widely.

"Don't be daft you would be lucky to get a card saying I wish you were here." Replied Helen jokingly.

Helen glanced over Aimee's shoulder and saw the picture of the beautiful shoes and matching clutch bag.

"IF and it is a big if, if I won loads of millions there is no way I would pay that amount of money for a pair of ankle breakers and a bag I could get only my lippy in."

"These are Jade's for the prom." Said Aimee turning around to her aunt. "Look how many likes she has, and she has put them on Instagram. She is so lucky don't you think Auntie Helen?"

"No love that is a picture from Sunday's paper magazine" replied Helen "couldn't tell you which magazine it was out off but the cost of shoes alone caused a lot of conversation especially with the cost of living at the moment."

Aimee frowned the page not quite believing and Kate smiled smugly.

Mum asked why there was a cause for celebration and Helen told them that she had bumped into an old school friend in town that afternoon.

"Get the glasses and I will tell you, but first Aimee I have Cousin Lucy's yellow dress here for you." Said Helen passing the dress to Aimee which was in a full-length zipped protector "Can I have a look at it on before I go, please."

Aimee did not want to put the dress on, she made an excuse that she hadn't showered, she was tired, and she would try it on the next day even though she had tried it on before. It was a beautiful, styled dress but in yellow …really.

"Auntie Helen has brought it specially so we can press it, go on try it on. Now love please "

Aimee took the dress bag and walked slowly to the stairs and climbed them heavily footed wishing she did not have to do this.

Suddenly there were screams coming from Aimee's bedroom everyone made a run for the stairs.

Mum threw the door open to see Aimee crying with delight as she held a Cadbury chocolate purple satin full length dress in her arms.

"What the heck" said Kate bulldozing her way into the bedroom and stroking the fabric which had tiny diamante crystals sewn on.

"Now I am no expert when it comes to frocks but that is a real champion frock" said dad proudly.

"FROCK" cried both girls in unison.

"A FROCK dad this is a gown," said Kate.

"It's gorgeous" sobbed Aimee with delight "I will try it on now."

They all trouped back downs stairs in disbelief.

"Helen how did you manage to get the dress it wasn't available to buy please tell me you haven't bought it from somewhere else as we shouldn't double up with the same gown" asked mum worriedly.

"My friend owns the bridal shop and she said she remembered you took a fancy to the Cadbury coloured dress and that unfortunately she couldn't sell it to you as someone had already chosen it and left a large non-refundable deposit."

Helen's friend told Helen that for the last few days she had been ringing the given mobile number and had left many messages and even tried to contact the mother on social media without success.

She had called at the house and there was no reply at the door and the neighbours said she thought they had gone away as she had not seen them.

Helen went on to tell them that her friend had closed the shop now as she was away for a few days and the dress hadn't been collected.

"So, to cut a long story short she asked me if you would still like the dress as she wouldn't be able to stock it until next year. So fortunately, the shop was a few minutes away, so we went to collect it."

The house phone rang sometime later in the evening which Dad answered and he came back into the room laughing.

"I do not believe this that was my mate who just rang and said he has found a stretched limo available if we still want one."

Aimee squealed with delight. "Ring him back dad and tell him yes" said Aimee bouncing across the room to her dad.

"It's a pink one" said dad quite uneasily and pulling a questionable face "will the lads be ok with that?"

Aimee rang her friends that were going originally, and she ran excitedly back into the lounge squealing.

"Dad, you wouldn't believe it the lads are more excited than the girls."

Mobile phones pinged as parents transferred money over to Aimee's parents accounts.

Aimee had a list of names and once paid she drew a line through the name excitedly.

A few parents called at the house to pay cash and were as excited as their children.

The day arrived all the leavers were having their photos taken.

"Get the limo in the shot" shouted out a male voice.

Dad went to speak to the driver who looked the part in his suit and chauffer hat. Mum went around the parents offering a small glass of fizz which was gladly taken.

The atmosphere was one of excitement and almost equal to a red-carpet film event. Shouts and squeals of delight off friends as they saw for the first-time their friends' dresses and suits.

Mobile phones clicking and photos flashing then being checked. The plastic glasses not quite making the clinking grade, it didn't matter. Everybody joined in even the neighbours came out to have a look at the young ladies in their refinery and not forgetting the lads all grown up in their hired suits.

Of course, the pink limo drew a lot of attention.

Outside Kilhey court all eyes and cameras were on the youngsters having their photo shoots for the local papers and school magazines

Kate went to over to Aimee.

"Aimee look over there on the car park."

Aimee looked in the direction Kate was hinting to look without pointing.

"WHAT THE?" Aimee looked at Kate and back at the small Fiat 500 which Jade was doing her best to struggle out of showing her white shoes and matching bag.

"Jade seems to have lost a little sparkle don't you think" Kate said quietly to Aimee.

Aimee threw her arms around Kate and gave her a hug.

"Kate I will never believe everything on social media again it was a definite learning curve, and I am so sorry for being so horrible."

"Go on gorgeous girl or you will miss your welcome drink and photos in the dining room" Kate replied holding back a small tear.

"Doesn't Aimee look so grown up in that frock," said her grandmother.

"FROCK! Mother it's a dress or even a ball gown I will have you know." Retorted Dad in an overly exaggerated posh voice

"Oh, my apologies son, and when did you become such an expert in ball gowns" She asked smiling up at her son who was walking her to her car.

"Mission accomplished" said Mum to Helen as they walked arm in arm "and it's with a big thanks to you Helen for getting that FROCK."

Their laughter could be heard all the way to the hall's grand doors.

Aimee blew the family a kiss and stepped confidently into Kilhey court to start the next chapter in her book of life.

Belle

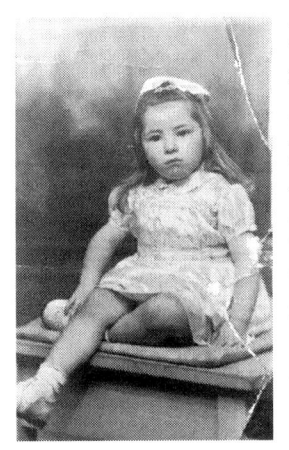

Belle woke early in the once familiar bed which now felt anything but. She stretched, a long cat like stretch, enjoying the feel of the luxurious Egyptian cotton sheets caressing her body. The house is quiet, apart from faint sounds coming from the large kitchen below her bedroom and there is a delicious smell of breakfast beginning to waft under the door.

Arabella, her full given name, arrived at Groven Hall late last night, to her relief everyone was in bed. Mrs Jacobs, housekeeper to the family for many years, had been pleased to see her and had embraced her warmly, much to Belle's surprise. Although it has been more than five years since Belle was last in her family's home, nothing has changed. Her room, still as it was when she left it under a cloud, in disgrace, whisked away in the small hours of the morning, without even saying goodbye to her siblings.

As Belle looks around at her childhood bedroom, the transition from innocent, happy go-lucky little girl who loved all things pink and fluffy to the young teenager full of hate and angst, who lived permanently under a black cloud, is clearly evident. The pink, cartoony wallpaper, now faded and in need of replacement remains under the many posters of heavy rock bands, lots of angry looking young men with dirty, matted hair, dressed in ripped clothing, adorned with many piercings and tattoos stare sadly down at her. The once white coving at the edge of the tall ceiling is now faded and in need of a lick of paint. She still recalls going with her beloved daddy to choose the ridiculously shaggy, white, expensive carpet that she now wriggles her toes in as she sits on the side of the bed. The shag pile is now looking as sad as Belle feels, flat in places and not white anymore, she can still see the dark stain where she spilt the black nail polish that she loved to wear, along with her dreary clothing and black eyeliner. Like the room's former occupant, the carpet has lost its bounce.

Belle stands and straightens the bedding, the crisp, white sheets still warm beneath her cold fingers, no change there, the house and her room is still as cold as ever. Just for a moment Belle is tempted to slip back under the lovely warm sheets and close her eyes, anything to avoid facing the family and today's ordeal. Instead, she smooths the wrinkles from the opulent pastel fabric of the handmade quilt as she steels herself to leave the room for breakfast. Belle feels a sense of deep sadness, she loved this beautiful safe room as a child, but now she hates everything about it, as she does the whole house. She retrieves all the stupid, tatty, fluffy stuffed animals from their resting place on the floor. Once loved and treasured, it had made Belle angry to see them artfully arranged on the bed last night, as if she was still a small child, and she had punched and kicked them to the floor in a rage.

2009 – The first time

2nd May, Arabella's 7th Birthday. It has been a fabulous day, spoiled rotten Arabella has had an extravagant, exciting party, it has just been the best day of her young life. The only daughter of her wealthy parents with older and younger brothers, Arabella is the apple of her parents and grandparents' eyes, especially her doting grandfather. Gramps, as only Arabella gets to call him, is her mother's father and the family all live together in his ancestral family home. Gramps is only soft with Arabella, CEO of the family business, he rules his family as he does the business, with a rod of iron.

Her grandmother, however, is vastly different from gramps. Arabella is convinced that her grandmother does not like her, certainly not like she likes the boys, particularly baby Hugo.

Grandmother seems to expect a lot from Arabella, in her young eyes anyway, she says girls must work harder than boys, harder and smarter. Grandmother loves to remind Arabella that she will not automatically go into the family business but must instead get educated and make her own way in the world, only then being allowed to join the company if she is up to it. As gramps rules the company grandmother is in charge in the home. To the community she is a pillar, school governor, head of the neighbourhood group, gives generously to local charities and community projects. Grandmother also loves to host garden parties for the community including the local school children, ruling the roost like queen bee. To the outside world Grandmother is a wonderful lady but since she first learned the word Belle has thought of her as 'the bitch.'

Its late, past her usual bedtime but Arabella was still excited and quite hyper after the eventful day. She has enjoyed being the centre of attention at the party, has eaten too many sweet things and really wanted to stay up later still to play with all her new gifts. Grandmother, tired from the day's events has instead sent Belle to bed with a slap on the leg, for being a spoilt, selfish little girl. Up in her bedroom Arabella sobs as quietly as she can, her head under her quilt to muffle her tears, now as miserable as she was happy just a fleeting time ago.

Her bedroom door creaks slightly as gramps peeps his head around it, a steaming mug in his hands.

"Hey pumpkin," his happy face always makes Belle smile, "come now, let's not end your lovely day with tears?"

"But gramps" Arabella sniffs as she sits upright in bed, pulling the sheet up to wipe her runny nose. "I wanted to play with my new things, I didn't want to go to bed yet!" "And besides" she continued "Jeremy is allowed to stay up, and he's not that much older than me!"

Gramps laughed, a lovely deep guffaw of a laugh that never failed to make Arabella laugh along with him, a small smile pulled at the corners of her rosebud like mouth.

"Now, now" he soothed, as he sat on the edge of the comfortable bed, "Jeremy is more than three years older than you and you know that you can never compete with him where your grandmother is concerned." "But my darling one, you will always be gramps favourite girl!" "Come on drink this warm milk, it will help you sleep." He handed her the now cooling mug of milk.

"Thanks gramps, Arabella sipped the warm soothing liquid, but it tasted funny. "Ew," she wrinkled her nose and tried to hand the mug back to her grandfather, "That tastes funny" she complains, "It tastes like flowers."

Her grandfather's demeanour and mood seem to shift as he pushes the mug back at her. "Don't be silly child, it's just milk, like you've had nearly every day of your life." His face softens slightly "it's probably the aftertaste of all the sweets you have eaten today, now drink up."

Arabella wraps both hands around the mug and drinks down the liquid without stopping, then hands her empty mug to gramps. "That's my girl" gramps smiles "now snuggle down and go to sleep." "Goodnight," he leaves the room quietly as Arabella's eyes begin to droop, and she sinks down, back under the cosy quilt, the sedative quickly taking effect.

Gramps feels a small sense of unease begin to creep into his conscience as he waits in his office down the hall from Arabella's bedroom, while the sedative he has mixed into her milk takes its full effect on his beautiful granddaughter.

Arabella drifted into a strange sleep, her body felt heavy, she tried to move her limbs, but it was if she was sinking in treacle. She thought that she heard her bedroom door open once again but her thoughts were so muddled and hazy, she could not be sure. By the time the early morning was peeking through her pink flowery curtains, Belle, thankfully, had forgotten what happened as she was drifting between sleep and wakefulness. she wonders however, why she recalls gramps face so close to hers that she could smell the stench of tobacco on his breath from those nasty cigars that he likes to smoke. Her memories are so muddled, and her head feels kind of fuzzy and odd. "I must have had a vivid dream" ponders Arabella as she thinks about gramps telling her to shush and pulling back her sheets.

12 May 2016 - Shame

Arabella is now an angry 15-year-old. Following the death of her beloved but weak father 3 years ago and as a result of the ongoing abuse at the hands of her once treasured grandfather, Arabella has become a sullen, snappy, rebellious teenager, unhappy with the world, her family and herself. Deserted by her father, neglected by her alcoholic mother, and hated by her grandmother, at one time she could always turn to her grandfather whom she could twist around her little finger but now she hated him. For years now gramps has been a regular visitor to her bedroom, when the house is asleep and no-one is watching, although Arabella knows that nobody cares anyway. No warm milk laced with sedatives anymore, gramps took to rubbing cocaine around her gums when Arabella was about ten, this method works more quickly and that means gramps does not have to wait. She knows now exactly what is happening to her, and the abuse has progressed over the years, but the coke takes the edge of things and Arabella now has a 'habit' which gramps funds for her. Gramps is good for that if nothing else, she knows that he will buy her whatever she needs or wants without question, a small price to pay for his pleasure.

I am sure that you are now thinking "why doesn't she tell someone?" well let me tell you, in the early days she tried. Her mother and grandmother scolded her for telling tales, the truth clearly too hard to face. Her poor father had taken the coward's way out.

Cute little Arabella was now unrecognisable. Gone are the pretty pink dresses, sweet pigtails, and glittery shoes, nowadays she dresses all in black, torn jeans and rock band t-shirts. Her hair has been cropped short and currently died purple but has been all shades of the rainbow. Her bedroom is now adorned with posters of the ugliest looking rock bands imaginable. She now longer goes to school, they tired of her constant antics and skipping lessons, she had become disruptive and rebellious. So, following her last suspension from the expensive private girls' school, the decision had been taken to provide her with a home tutor, who came to the house daily, but Arabella was resistant to learn.

It's Saturday night and the family are entertaining, a charity dinner with all the local bigwigs and do-gooders being wined and dined and persuaded to part with substantial amounts of cash, for a worthy cause of cause.

Belle, as she now likes to be called, is, as usual up in her room, listening to rock music and texting the mates, who she plans to sneak out to meet just as soon as the party gets under way.

Belle loves hanging out with her new mates, and they love her, especially when gramps supplies her with coke, they loved to get high together. The family, however, do not approve of the company she now keeps, but Belle does not care about that and gets out to hang out with her friends whenever she can get past the gate keeper aka 'the bitch.'

Its 8.30 now and the party now seems to be in full swing, time to get ready for a night of fun. As she comes out of the shower, her hair in a towel, Belle feels a kind of cramp like flutter in her abdomen. "ooh" she sucks in her breath as she bends forward trying to relieve the discomfort "that's odd, period pains?" "I hope not" thinks Belle, she has been getting close to one of the older guys in the group, Jonathon, and she was hoping to 'move things up a level" tonight.

As Belle sat and applied her pale make up and black eye liner, she tried not to think about the now increasing pain that was gripping her, concentrating instead on perfecting 'her look!'

She pops her freshly laundered t-shirt over her head, pulling it down over the soft curves of her shapely breast, smoothing it over her round, paunchy little muffin top, the lovely benefits of a home with staff, she always had freshly laundered clothes. Next Belle picks out her favourite black, ripped jeans, "fit for nothing but the dustbin" according to her grandmother! "Ha, what does she know, the old bitch" Belle laughs to her empty room. "Whoa, these have got a bit tight" Belle lies almost flat on the bed to pull the zipper up on her skinny jeans, letting out a long breath as the zipper reaches the waistband. "Really must cut down on the junk food" Belle chuckles to herself.

As Belle stands to look at her image in the full-length mirror attached to her bedroom door, the pain suddenly intensifies, she lets out a loud yelp as she doubles over in distress. Beads of sweat now begin the form on her brow as Belle, nausea overtaking her, crumbles to the floor, griping, crushing waves of agony squeezing her abdomen, she screams louder now, unable to control what is happening to her.

The bedroom door opens, and her mother stands at the entrance, hands on hips. "Arabella, what on earth is going on in here?" she takes a couple of tentative steps into the room. "Your grandmother sent me to check on you, to make sure that you were not planning on sneaking out, which you obviously were, but what the hell is wrong with you? what are you screaming about?"

Arabella's pain is now out of control. She is clawing her way up onto the bed.

"Arabella, what are you playing at? Why have you wet your pants?

Distraught Arabella could do nothing but cry, scream and writhe in agony, not caring that she was now wet through, while she tried desperately to get out of her tight jeans.

"Mum" she cried out in desperation "Help me, please, get my jeans off me, it hurts so much, what is happening to me?"

Her mother, repelled by the scene unfolding in her daughter's bedroom flees from the room.

Within what seemed like seconds Arabella's room is filled with people, grandmother is taking charge and barking orders at Mrs Jacobs, Molly, the maid, Stephanie, her brother's girlfriend, and Dr Barton, "How did he get here so fast" wondered Belle through her pulsating pains.

As Steph and grandmother manage to pull her sodden jeans off Belle's legs, she feels an overwhelming urge originating somewhere in her abdomen, to push. Grandmother stands back, aghast, in shock, as the baby's head, covered in thick dark hair emerges, followed quickly by its tiny body.

The baby makes no sound as it is wrapped in a clean fluffy towel and whisked away.

Three days later, Belle is herself whisked away, in the early hours of the morning. Without even chance to say goodbye to her siblings Belle is sent to a boarding school for wayward girls, that is, after being told that her baby was stillborn.

The Will – present day

The solum breakfast in the drawing room with her estranged family was difficult, having not seen most of them for years. However, Belle was delighted to meet her adorable niece, the only child of her elder brother Jeremy and his now wife Stephanie. Their wedding had been a low key, hurried affair, Belle was not invited to attend, and as gorgeous Emily had been born not long after the wedding she understood why. Hmm "double standards" mused Belle at the time she was informed of her niece's birth, but that was no surprise as grandmother adored her brothers and Stephanie had virtually taken residence up grandmothers' backside, fawning over her at every opportunity.

Being the black sheep of the family, Belle had been kept at her prison aka boarding school until today. She could have attended her grandfather's funeral six weeks ago, but she had refused to go, under the circumstances.

Little Emily was the only ray of sunshine at breakfast. She entered the drawing room holding her father's hand. Belle was dazzled, she did not think that she had ever seen such a beautiful child, tall and slender with long golden hair framing her gorgeous round race dotted with freckles and sporting the cutest dimples.

"Hello there sweetie" Belle pulled out a chair alongside her own "Come and sit next to auntie Belle, Emily, and tell me all about you" Emily flashed Belle the most enigmatic smile as she went to climb up to the seat next to her.

"Emily" her brother Jeremy barked as he once again took hold of his daughter's hand. "Come over here and sit in your seat next to your great grandmother" Emily sadly slunk over to the designated chair as Belle's grandmother shot her a look of pure triumph.

"Sit down Emily and eat your breakfast" grandmother pushed the child's chair into the table as a plate of food was placed in front of her. "Aunt Belle is too busy, she has no time to 'get to know you,' she will be leaving again very soon. Belles' adorable niece grinned across the table at her from behind the curtain of silky blonde curls.

Once the awkward breakfast was over the family assembled in grandfather's study for the reading of his will. The study was formerly out of bounds for pretty much everyone but grandfather, Belle was intrigued to finally go inside.

The forbidden room, like the rest of the house, has a tall ceiling, cobwebs clustered in most of the corners, even the maid wasn't allowed in. The smell of grandfather's cigar smoke still hangs in the air mixed with a stale mustiness and the rich odour of old leather from the now tatty green chesterfield couches around the room. One of the couches, once shiny and beautiful but now dull and cracked with years of old men sitting on it while they drank grandfather's expensive brandy and smoked his Cuban cigars, is facing his desk, where the family are now seated. The large old desk, which grandfather sat behind in his wing-backed chair takes centre stage in the stale smelling room, in front of the large bay window. Glorious sunshine poured in through the eight-foot-wide window, which offers sumptuous views of the magnificent garden, resplendent with its emerald green, immaculately stripped lawns surrounded by deep borders filled with unusual, exotic ornamental plants. Mr Forsyth, the family's solicitor sits awkwardly in the tall chair, a halo of light around him, making him look like a crusty of angel, Belle stifled a giggle. He leans forward, as Belle takes her seat, to shuffle the papers gathered on the well-worn mahogany desk, topped with leather, now beginning to curl at the edges, his desk had seen better days.

Belle, is still unsure why she has been called to this reading, clearly, she must be named in the will, surely her grandfather has not left her anything of value?

Belle is not paying much attention to what the old solicitor is saying, blah blah blah, she is wondering instead about her gorgeous little niece, or not so little, she seems very tall and well-spoken for her age. The rest of the family however seem to be on the edge of their seats, waiting like vultures, to pick over the spoils.

"NO, oh no" cries her mother. Belle is now paying more attention, her grandmother has her hand clasped across her mouth, the colour all drained from her face, Belle is convinced she is about to faint. The family all seem to be talking at once, loudly, and very animated.

"Arabella" Mr Forsyth is looking impatiently at her, obviously waiting for a response. "Did you hear what I said?"

"Er no sorry" Belle is beginning to feel uneasy, what on earth is happening, her mother is now crying noisily!

"Apart from the house and the business, your grandfather has left his entire fortune to you, current estimate £175,000,000, along with the instruction to give you this envelope. He hands Belle a small envelope emblazoned with her full name, in her grandfather's handwriting.

Belle struggles to compose herself, astounded at the news she has just been given. She feels an odd urge to burst into hysterical laughter. The family around her, however, are doing anything but laugh, Belle blocks out their protests of "not fair" "I don't believe it" etc as she pulls the creased paper from its envelope.

The only words written on the notepaper in her grandfather's pen are "I'm sorry." Hah, so you bloody should be! Belle is just about to throw the note and envelope in the bin when she notices that there is another piece of paper, she retrieves is curious.

It is her daughter's birth certificate:

Child's name – Emily Arabella Groven

Father – William Hugo Groven Mother – Arabella Jade Groven

Date of Birth – 12 May 2016

Spreading My Wings ...
@ The Comfy Nest

Allow me to introduce Aunty Maud, the beautiful lady in the picture, when she was a young woman in her prime. I was fortunate to meet her at a place called "The Cosy Nest", a home for retired gentlefolk.

You see when I popped out of my shell, my cosy nest was surrounded by beautiful pink cherry blossom in the cherry tree in the garden of said nursing home. It was absolutely beautiful; I could hear chirping and singing there were six little open beaks who I now know were my brothers and sisters. They were waiting for dad bringing home the food, a few worms to bring us all on till we were big enough to fly the nest. Naturally I took my place at the table and over the weeks grew stronger until dad started saying that we needed to think about leaving the nest.

Well, that's another story, I'm terrified of heights, sounds funny from a bird, doesn't it? All my siblings took to it like a duck to water if you'll excuse my pun, but me, well, I was the last in the nest because every time it came to my turn, I chickened out. Everyone had left ... Each day I took a few steps to the edge of the nest, and everything started spinning. The next thing I knew I was surrounded by furry stuff, it was quite snug but not like the nest, I could hear someone singing but this time it was a human! I popped my head out of the new nest and looked up, I could see lots of grey hair cascading down the fur, then I realised I was in someone's pocket ... Eeek!

"Oh Hello, I wondered when you would wake up", said Maud in a lovely soft voice.

"How did I get here, I'm frightened of flying", I said to Aunt Maud sitting next to me.

I wondered what advice she could give me for my problem. I don't know why but I knew she felt my fear so understood even though she didn't speak fluent bird!!!

Or would she maybe guide me over to the windowsill and entice me to climb on it - open the window and wait for me to fly, in my mind I was terrified and prayed to God that was not the case.

She can just keep me in her room and feed me bread and things I thought, I loved it in her warm dressing gown pocket, I would poke my little head out and sing to her, her kind eyes peering down over her glasses.

Well, she did take me to the windowsill and indeed opened the window. But then she just encouraged me sit there and contemplate.

All I could feel was my fear rising into my throat and almost spilling from my beak, but I hung on to that fear for dear life, as it was the only thing holding me together at that moment in time.

I could not even look down over the sill because you see I'm terrified of heights – not a great trait for a bird, especially an overweight bird - is it?

Don't do it, don't do it…. oh yes, I have an inner *VOICE* and I've named her my *'WHAT IF BIRD'* she's the bane of my life. She constantly squawks if I try to go out of my comfort zone. You'll only fail and then you look so stupid, stay where it's safe.

Hence, I hop everywhere slowly! It's so knackering hopping. So, wish I could fly and then I wouldn't be weird and could find some mates.

I look at Aunt Maud again and she is just sat looking very thoughtful as though she's trying to find a solution for my dilemma. I study her face and think to myself even though her face is full of wrinkles and laughter lines she's quite beautiful and I could see from her picture, a stunner in her hay day. Every wrinkle and laughter line could tell a story of its own I'm sure, I bet she has led a full and productive life. I think I could sit on this windowsill and listen to her talk for hours and hours.

However, she has other ideas....

Suddenly she stands and starts to stroke my feathers. I start to relax and push my head into her hand so she can stroke a certain spot. All of a sudden, I'm involuntarily moving towards the edge of the windowsill, and I can't stop myself. My 'What If Bird' is going flippin mental! Screaming STOP, STOP, STOP - but I can't.

I suddenly stop, only managing to teeter on the edge by clinging with my little claws for dear life. Maud quietly whispers in a gentle voice,

"What's the worst that could happen bird - if you stepped off?"

I told her how crazy she was, in my head I was thinking - I'll die. Then she said ever, ever so quietly

"Let's see if that's true then" - and without further ado, she gave me a gentle but forceful push and I was off the flippin sill with nothing below me but the fear my imminent death. At this point I think my 'What If Bird' had passed out from its own fear of being out of a job.

Then to my amazement I started to flap my little wings and the harder I tried the higher I flew. I kept chanting to myself "flap baby flap you CAN do this" and it was so helpful not having that negative voice telling me …

"You can't do it – you'll just fail as always"

But now I really knew what it felt like to fly, and I was exhilarated and could not believe my own eyes …

I'd actually done it.

That night as I lay in my comfortable nest, I realised what can seem like a cruel and sneaky act, was in fact the only thing that ever made me fly. I so wanted to tell Maud - thank you, thank you and thank you again.

Well, it's two weeks now since Aunty Maud enabled me to trust my own abilities. So, I've now spread my wings. My little wings are so much stronger now and I've been practicing flying around the Comfy Nest Garden and I'm improving hour by hour, Aunt Maud says so.

I'm also much better at providing myself with food from the garden and not just relying on Aunty Mauds generosity for titbits however she's stills leaves out snacks for me on her windowsill every day, I love her so much.

I've found all sorts of tasty food around the cherry tree and other areas of the garden.

Hidden from sight there is a great big mound of rotting stuff that looks like soil buts its different and the garden-man chops and digs it into a mush then he mixes other stuff with it. He then goes away leaves it before eventually spreading it into the flower beds. Such disgusting stuff, it absolutely stinks nevertheless it's worth the horrible smell because there are great big fat juicy worms hiding in it. So, when the man goes for his lunch, I go for mine and nab a couple or three of those juicy worms for my lunch, yum, yum!

However, there's something keeps knocking on my birdie brain and telling me it's time to move on from this garden and find a different place to grow up, find a lady bird and raise my own babies. I don't understand why but I know it's the right thing to do and sooner rather than later, just like all my birdie siblings did plus my Mum and Dad have disappeared, and I don't suppose I'll see them again! But how do I tell Aunty Maud after she's been so good to me, without hurting her feelings. I will miss her so much.

Anyway, it's time for my daily visit to see Aunty Maud. I've actually missed her these last few afternoons she's not been there, and her window has been closed, maybe she gone shopping with Doris from room 6, they are the best of friends.

The very next day, I saw the open window and perched on the edge of the nest, I cricked my neck as I tried to see her. There were two carers chatting ...

"It will be funny not having Maud here, she was such a lovely soul, hopefully she will be with her husband now in paradise"

I felt a tear well up inside me as I looked up to the Heavens ... She passed away peacefully in her sleep the previous night.

Thankyou Maud my lovely friend.

I truly believe this wasn't her first time of helping someone find their confidence and self believe and maybe had a bit of fun when pushing me off!!!

I bet wherever she is now she's helping others FLY in whatever capacity they may need.

So, from my point of view and to look at it positively - the bravery of the Maud taught me a brilliant lesson.

I can do anything I put my mind to if only I trust myself and don't listen to other's negativity. Failing is not a mistake, but a learning experience.

Anyway, I'm signing off … See ya, I'm needing to spread my wings further afield now.

Diggle Junction

As the 6 O'clock to Crewe approached the unfinished station platform, suddenly, a cry of Dad! rang out. Larry was lost in the moment ...

"Dad are you deaf or daft?" called out Jon, Larry's 13-year-old son. His peace broken; his attention brought swiftly back to the present.

"Have you forgotten; I've got athletics tonight; I need to get going!" said Jon as he flung open the shed door looking frustrated, and from the sense of urgency anyone would think it was life and death thought Larry. It was his only outlet, working on his beloved 00-gauge model railway at the bottom of the garden in his man cave. It was affectionately known as Diggle Junction, it was his peaceful place, his sanctuary.

"Where's your mother, I suppose she's on the bloody phone, chatting as usual!"

He banged his paint brush on the bench and spilled khaki green all over the newly laid grassy area on the banking of his latest track extension. "Shit!", frustration spilling over, he slammed the shed door shut and followed Jon up to the house. Another 20-mile round trip, another wasted couple of hours ... A continuous merry go round which he dares not disembark. In his mind, the only way was down, crash and burn! Since he turned forty, Larry's life seemed to have taken a nosedive, he had been finished from his job 6 months ago on ill health and is filling in time in a dead-end job simply to keep the house open. It was impossible for him to stay on the sick and had accepted just any job, simply to keep the roof over their heads. In reality, he wasn't fit to return to work and the twelve hours back-to-back shifts are taking their toll, he feels constantly exhausted.

He sauntered through the house, picked up his car keys and nodded to Helen who as he had predicted, was scrolling through social media.

It took her the best part of 5 minutes to raise her head "See ya later", she called as he was almost through the door. As Larry closed the front door, he noticed a young woman walking very purposefully down the avenue, looking at the houses inquiringly. She was 'attached' to her mobile ... 'on autopilot' Larry thought, then she lifted her head just as he sat in the driver seat and their eyes connected, her face evoked a memory, but he just couldn't put his finger on who she was. The young woman, a half-smile emerging looked as if she knew Larry, she stood momentarily looking over.

Jon was already installed in the car preoccupied with ping … ping!

He had more conversations with virtual friends than real humans these days, especially the very person who was working his socks off keeping everyone in the style they were accustomed to, Larry thought. I'm like a well-worn overcoat, falling apart at the seams.

He enquired if Jon knew the young woman he had seen as they left, somehow, she had left an indelible print on his mind. Jon seemed to think he had seen her coming out of the flat over the newsagents, maybe she was the new tenant? The journey to the athletics track took best part of 40 minutes, the conversation was muted, mostly one way and with one-word answers from Jon. Larry's mind was elsewhere, he had a Hawk moth character living in his head who opened his wings on every occasion to tell him how bad things were, there in the abyss between the family and work, Oh … and Diggle Junction.

Jon was chatting to his mate Peter on What's App, quite oblivious of the muted conversation in the car, he had been telling Peter how great his dad was running him here and there and how he didn't know what he would do without dad's taxi. Jon confided in his friend that he was quite worried about his dad, he seemed so distant and difficult to connect with. He had become more reliant on him because mum was always busy 'influencing' making beauty videos and trying to grow her followers on Instagram as well as watching soaps, Love Island and scrolling on other social media sites. I don't know who she's influencing, he informed Peter, it's definitely not dad, he even has to get his own tea when she's been home all day.

Arriving at the track, Jon grabbed his bag and jumped out of the car.

"A couple of hours dad, so pick me up around eight please, can I have a takeaway on the way back?"

As he turned left to start the drive back, he noticed the light sandstone façade of Mossley Railway Station looking resplendent in the evening sunshine. He loved everything about railways and decided to stop and wait for Jon and take a look round. Before long, he found himself sat under wooden shelter on the platform, there were a few people milling about waiting for the next train and a lady tending to some plants on a grassy bank at the side of the waiting room. Larry was bewitched by all the beautiful colours of the geraniums, marigolds and other bedding covering the scrubland, great work he thought.

It was peaceful taking in the atmosphere once the next train had lifted all the passengers off the platform and left him alone with his thoughts. He felt a sense of sadness and sat with his head in his hands for a minute, it dawned on him that he was feeling flat and unmotivated, couldn't quite put his finger on it. Sitting up and leaning back into the bench, he closed his eyes and drifted into a dreamworld, hypnotised by the sound of the birds, not a click or ping in range. He wondered if Helen was still scrolling and if she would miss him if he didn't return, probably not he thought …

Would they miss him at the flour plant, if he wasn't packing, all those 2 kgs bags of self-raising, piling up off the end of the line, making a mountain of white stuff as the bags burst open and dispersed into the air, probably not and to be honest, he didn't care, he was just a number, they would replace him with another mug …

What about Jon? Would he miss him? No lifts, walking to school, no takeaways, no pocket money, no new trainers, fancy jackets, and designer shirts … possibly!

The station Tanoy brought him back to the present, announcing the next train approaching, he locked eyes with the train driver as he pulled slowly into the station on the opposite platform. Another announcement … The next train on platform five is the TransPennine Express, please stand back behind the yellow line … Suddenly, his attention was captured by a young man standing a metre in front of him, he was precariously close to the edge, triggering an automatic response … he walked towards the lad and shouted to him just as the 19.20 express flew through the station sounding as if a thousand horses had galloped past.

"Mate, stand back!" Larry's heart was racing, sweat was pouring from his brow, envisioning a tragedy, silent tears began to well up inside him

"Yeah, I'm fine thanks, although I'm not sure about you, have you seen a ghost?"

"No, I'm all good thanks, sorry, didn't mean to spook you, my mind was elsewhere, I saw the train, then I saw you and somehow thought you might get pulled over the edge"

They shook hands and parted ways, Larry took some deep breaths which seemed to calm him, looking at his watch, he realised it had been a good hour since he left Jon and thought he might return to the track and see if he could catch the back end of training.

 As he was leaving, he bumped into the gardening lady with her tools,

"You've done a great job there!" he remarked as she passed. He took a second look as she walked in front of him, her long brunette hair tied into a ponytail swinging as she strolled out of the station. Mmm … he thought, very nice, then remembered Helen at home. He was telling himself off for admiring the female form floating gracefully in front of him, his father's words came to mind … well, even if you own a restaurant, you're allowed to look at someone else's menu! The memory triggered a broad smile. For a brief interlude, he had forgotten his low mood and intrusive thoughts.

His heart rate had returned to normal as he walked into the arena where Jon was in the process of running a 100-metre sprint. As he crossed the line, he gave a punch to the air, a victory salute, a sense of achievement. He turned and saw his dad stood alone on the edge of the track, ran over, giving a warm hug, he announced:

"Personal best! so glad you were here to see it dad, I think I'll be picked for the county meet next month"

"Proud of you son!"

Larry felt guilty, he had not stayed to watch training, but his motivation was on the floor just now and he had overlooked the fact that Jon might after all like his dad to be involved.

The Hawk moth in his head took over, "You're a waste of time Larry, fancy not even going to watch Jon when he's doing so well. What sort of dad are you? You're selfish! You don't deserve to be a dad. Waste of space. Waste of Breath, and everything else!"

Larry held Jon who was still mid hug, he stifled back the tears and vowed in his mind, he would try to pull himself together … soon.

In the car on the way home, Jon dropped off, he was obviously exhausted from the session and adrenaline hit. Five minutes from home Larry pulled into the drive through and got Jon's favourite burger meal, much to the boy's surprise.

As they walked into the house, there was a beautiful aroma of an Italian restaurant, the sweet smell of garlic and Italian herbs wafted through the hall.

Helen appeared from the kitchen, "Ah, you're back, I've made a pasta bake and garlic bread" Larry was dropped on …

"Certainly, smells the part" he remarked.

The table was set with cutlery and two wine glasses, Helen had read his mind and not cooked for Jon who she knew instinctively would be catered for already.

"I thought we might eat at the table and have a glass of wine whilst it's Friday and no work tomorrow, we hardly ever have a conversation these days"

Larry nodded in agreement,

Before the first glug of wine had hit the glass and contrary to the cordial atmosphere, Helen snarled "You're so distant Larry, how have we got to this, I thought all would be well after changing jobs but, you don't seem interested"

He gave a shrug and remained expressionless, he could feel those dreaded tears emerging like a tidal wave, he had to walk away. In his mind, Helen simply didn't understand, she had no idea and seemed to be getting on with her life, thanks very much. Helen was angry, she felt dejected after she had made all this effort, the air rained with obscenities, he was a selfish pig anyway, only interested in that damn model railway!

"I'm off!" he barked "Should have known it was too good to be true, you are making an effort instead of ping ping ping ... chat chat chat!"

She brushed off his complaint with a dismissive wave of her hand ... Blah Blah Blah she sang as she turned and walked away.

Larry once again found himself at Diggle Junction with the door slammed firmly behind him. In despair he reached for a small bottle of Whisky he kept there ... only for medicinal purposes. He sensed the Hawk moth re-appearing, "They would be better off without you Larry. She doesn't care about you. You would be better off out of it. It makes sense, you would be better off dead!"

He reached for the previous Friday's copy of the Evening Standard which he had stashed down the side of his worktable and, unrolled it ... slowly.

Inquest opens into death of 51-year-old struck by train in Dewsbury

Assistant West Yorkshire coroner David Martin opened an inquest into the death of James Nolan, 51, in August last year. He confirmed the medical cause of death as multiple head and chest injuries sustained in a collision with a train.

Train driver Larry Salmons provided a written statement to the inquest with an account of the tragic accident. The coroner recorded a verdict of suicide...

If you have been affected by the issues raised in this story and would like to speak to someone about it, contact The Samaritans on 116 123 or visit www.samaritans.org/how-we-can-help/contact-samaritans

As he read the report for the 20th time, the face of the young woman whom he saw earlier hit him dawning on him, she was the daughter of James Nolan. He knew it was his nemesis, but how to come to terms with himself, he had no idea. Feelings of despair filled his space; he had seen the ashen looks on the faces of James' family at the coroner's court and felt an overwhelming guilt but there was nothing he could have done. A tsunami of tears flowed as Larry remembered, it was simply a waterfall which could not be controlled. He was sobbing loudly as Helen walked down the garden path to the shed. As she approached the door, through the sobbing, she heard Larry saying …

"Is that the Samaritans? I really need help; I killed a man"

Helen ran to open the door, saw him sat there in despair. He hardly noticed as she sat beside him and hugged him as tight as she could. "Larry, I'm here love, you're not alone, we can work this out … together".

He crumbled in her arms, lost in the moment, Helen took the phone from him and spoke to the person on the other end, terminating the conversation. She whispered to him in calming tones and held him till he managed to compose himself. He needed closure then maybe he could get back into the real world and live his life again.

Over the next few days Larry discussed with Helen how he had seen the daughter of James Nolan at the coroner's court and again in the street as her was taking Jon to the athletics meet. The information from the coroner's hearing which was whirling around his head like a tornado, mangling his thoughts into unfathomable drivel. A verdict of suicide which wasn't enough to reassure Larry, and to compute that he was not responsible, a man's life snuffed out in heartbeat on a busy railway line. Life was so cruel, a life that was immeasurably happy before the incident, what must James' family think of him driving the train which wiped out his precious life? Larry couldn't get his head round it; he was drowning in an ocean of guilt and foreboding. The simple word "suicide" was too inferior to describe what had happened and Larry felt sad that he had not known James and been able to prevent him taking his own life.

If only James had known the devastation he would leave behind, both in his own family and in the families of others who would be dragged into the drama. For the first time in his life, Larry had considered taking *his* own life as a result of the mental torment he was suffering. Helen was grateful that her sweetheart was opening up, she had not realised how deeply he was affected by the loss of life and the loss of his beloved job as a train driver.

The fog of grief seemed to lift slowly as he worked through his feelings with his newly appointed counsellor at the local clinic. He kept looking out for the young woman whom he thought was James' daughter, she had dissolved into the ether just as quickly as she had appeared. He wanted her to know how sorry he was, just a few words …

The Yellow Raincoat

She gave me one, last, withering, look, as she walked out of the door, and into the raging storm." Well, I am going to find him" were my headstrong daughter's parting words, seconds before she slammed the front door behind her. Oh, how quickly life can change, how alarmingly fast can circumstances deteriorate and turn things upside down, especially when you have a child like Alice. Determined, beautiful, whirlwind Alice, the paediatric consultants have yet to give a definite diagnosis, but she certainly sings from a different song sheet from the rest of us, with all her dos and don'ts and funny little quirks, but hey, that's what makes her our special little girl.

We had been having a lovely afternoon despite the storm raging outside. Alice had been playing happily with her baby brother Ben, when the doorbell rang to announce the arrival of the postman. Eight-year-old Alice could now reach to open the front door, even though she had been told so many times not to answer the door unless it was someone we knew and allowed her to. On this occasion, as I knew it was our "friendly local postman Jack, I allowed her to open the door.

"Mummy, mummy, look, it's from Grandma" my daughter's eyes shone with excitement, as she

was already tearing into the neatly wrapped brown paper parcel. "Grandma promised me that she was sending presents, can I open mine mummy please?", inside the parcel were two separately wrapped presents in pretty, thick, expensive looking wrapping paper. The gift decorated with little girls in pink tutus and shiny ballet shoes tied with pink ribbon and a bow, was clearly for Alice.

"Yes of course, Grandma will be delighted that she has made you so happy" I grin as I reply, although my answer is clearly mute as Alice already has the parcel unwrapped before I have finished speaking.

I pick up the present who's wrapping is adorned with dinosaurs of every different size and colour, mum certainly knows her grandchildren, Ben is currently obsessed with all things dino, and hand it to Ben.

Two-year-old Ben is the complete opposite to his sister, easy going, and always pleasant, he is my happy smiley baby. He takes his gift eagerly with his chubby little hands, the dimples in his round cheeks evident as he smiles broadly at me, he begins to unwrap his surprise.

Alice by now is becoming animated, jumping up and down with sheer delight, her hands flapping rapidly.

"She remembered, mummy, grandma remembered!"

Her glee is contagious, and I find myself grinning along with her, as Alice opens out the sweet little yellow raincoat with seven duck shaped buttons down the front and matching weatherproof hat, complete with duck face.

"Of course, she did darling, grandma promised you a yellow raincoat to match hers, and you know grandma always keeps her promises"

Good old mum, I think to myself, she always comes through with the most perfect gifts. I make a mental note to telephone to thank her later. Ben meanwhile is attempting to try on the colourful dinosaur sweater that mum has obviously knitted for him. I turn to help, as he is trying to pull it up over his legs.

"Mummy, fasten my buttons please, mummy", Alice is hopping from one leg to another, impatient as always, the buttons a little too tricky for her small fingers. She is now dressed in the smart new coat; a grin splits her face from ear to ear as she struggles to contain herself. The duck hat is perched on her head, the ties dangling by her ears.

"You don't need it fastened right now Alice"

I sit back and look at my spirited little girl, as Ben proudly parades around the room in his new sweater. "We are not going out today, look at the weather", I part the blinds so that she can see the wild storm outside. The rain is bouncing down on the road outside the window, running like a river down to the stream at the end of the road, the trees twist and bend as the wind whips them ferociously.

"You only need to try it on today, Alice, it is far too wet and windy to go out", I wait for her to protest, as I know she will, Alice does not like to be told no, and if she has a coat on then it must be fastened, just one of her ways. I relent and lean over to fasten her buttons; she does look adorable in the bright yellow PVC.

"But mummy" she exclaims, "what about meeting daddy from the bus, we always meet daddy from the bus!"

This is generally true as Alice loves to go and meet her father when he arrives home from his day in the office, and I usually indulge her.

"Oh sweetheart, daddy won't mind if we don't meet him today, it is far too wet and windy for all three of us to go out today"

My answer is obviously common sense, but I hold my breath as I await my daughter's response to my refusal.

"And besides honey", I continue, before she has chance to open her mouth, daddy is going to be late tonight". I stand as she looks crestfallen.

"now", I continue, as I open the kitchen door, "why don't you come and help me get dinner ready for daddy"

She usually likes to help in the kitchen. "We can make him a nice stew to warm him up when he comes in". I am hoping that peeling carrots and potatoes will help keep her mind off going outside.

Alice, for once dutifully follows me to the kitchen, still of course wearing her yellow raincoat, the duck hat perched upon her blonde untamed curls.

"I will peel the carrots mummy", she announces as she pulls her step stool over to the countertop. Now some people may think eight is very young to be handling a sharp veg peeler, but Alice is ultra precise in every task she undertakes and is very aware of sharp implements and how to use them correctly. Ben follows his big sister to see what is going on, I deposit him in his highchair close to me and give him a carrot to chew on. Alice peels the carrots at the speed of lightning and is now again hopping from one foot to another, something clearly on her mind.

"Ben, be careful with that raw carrot, you might choke", as I said she is ultra safety conscious.

"Mummy, it's not safe for Ben, he may choke", my unpredictable daughter is becoming agitated, practically jumping up and down on her step, her hat bobbing up and down on her head.

"Mummy, it's getting late", yes, she can tell the time, unfortunately sometimes, I am constantly reminded what time it is and what time we need to go to school etc.

"Yes Alice, it's okay" I hug her trying to reassure her, "Ben is fine, mummy is watching him"

I lean over and take any small pieces of carrot off my son's highchair tray.

"Don't worry about the time sweetheart, daddy will be home soon I am sure". My efforts to pacify Alice's worries are obviously not working, as she jumps down from the step and goes over to her brother. The next few moments happen in a blur. Alice is shouting at me "mummy, get your coat on, we need to go and meet daddy. It is very late", she is now reaching up to lift Ben from his chair. "I will get Ben's coat on mummy, while you get ready", Ben stands up in his chair eager to reach

his sister's arms, Alice not quite tall enough to lift him up and over puts her arms under his armpits and pulls him forward. I drop my knife and reach out, but I am too late, both children and the chair topple onto the kitchen floor, with a loud, sickening thud.

Ben's scream pierces the air as his head crashes against the cupboard, his loud sobs fill the room. Alice, seemingly unhurt, jumps to her feet, rushes to the hall, and pulls out her wellington boots, oblivious to the chaos she has left in the kitchen.

"Alice, what are you doing? Ben, darling, it's okay, you will be okay" I comfort my son in my arms, I can see a large bruise forming above his left eye but otherwise he seems intact. I am sitting cross-legged on the cold floor, Ben's cry still ringing in my ears.

"Mummy" my daughter yells, "we need to find daddy now".

"Alice, no, daddy will be fine" my patience is beginning to wear thin. "Ben is hurt, and he needs a cuddle, not to go out in this storm".

Alice, now fully dressed in her coat, hat and yellow wellingtons, shot me her final, defiant look as she slammed out of the door.

My daughter can be quite sensible, but as the storm rages outside, the panic wells up inside and threats to overtake me. I scooped Ben up from the floor, his sobs now subsiding, he whimpers as I push his little arms into his coat, and pull up his hood, no time for shoes, I will carry him. I ram my own feet into a pair of slippers, nearest footwear to hand and yank opens the front door. The rain has eased slightly, but the wind is quite ferocious, and it whips my long hair across my face, blurring my vision. My stomach is doing somersaults as I scurry down the street, searching for my errant daughter. My unease increases as I realise Alice is already out of sight. It's not far to the bus stop on the high street but we need to go over the small bridge that crosses the stream, maybe she is waiting at the bridge for me, Alice doesn't like crossing the bridge by herself, I can feel my heart thud in my chest as I hope that I am right. I am moving as fast as I can, but the path is strewn with fallen leaves which now they are wet have become sodden and slippery. My feet, in their unsuitable footwear slip and slide on the

treacherous surface, my rising panic hampering my progress further. I reach out to grab something, anything, as the ground seems to slip from under me. My hand clutches at thin air, as my legs, seeming to have a mind of their own go way, in two separate directions. Fortunately,

I managed to clasp Ben to my bosom as I land unceremoniously on my bottom in the muddy foliage.

No time to check what damage I might have done, I scrabble to my feet, Ben's chubby little hands wound tightly around my neck, we make our way over to the small bridge. I can feel a large damp patch chilling my rear end, and I am now aware of a significant graze to my right hand, I must have caught it as I tried to slow my fall, I can feel the tears forming behind my eyes.

My hopes dashed, my heart sinks as we approach the bridge and I realise Alice is still nowhere in sight, she must have overcome her fear and crossed the rickety wooden structure, desperate to reach her beloved daddy.

Off the slippery leaves, I am moving quicker now, as I realise that Alice will be on the busy high street, looking for the bus stop where her father alights. As I reach the centre of the small bridge

a strong gust of wind sweeps across from the water, making me lose my balance slightly. I grasp the wet handrail, turning towards the gushing torrent of water below, struggling to stay upright while keeping my son safe in my arms. The torrential downpour had turned the usually quiet

stream into a gurgling, cascading flow, bits of leaves and twigs spinning and twirling as they hurry by, the water level so high it's threatening to break the banks. Holding on to the barrier with one hand, the other firmly around Ben, my hair wildly blowing around my face, a flash of bright yellow catches my eye in the stream below.

I slither down over the remainder of the bridge and down on to the banking to get a better look fear welling up inside, threatening to consume me. I can see it clearly now, a bright yellow duck hat, is swirling and spinning in the fast-flowing cascade.

My legs buckle, as I fall to my knees in the muddy, wet grass, bile rises in my throat, the urge to vomit overwhelming. I hear the high-pitched wail before I even realise that my mouth is open. Tears now spill over as the realization engulfs me.

"Alice, oh Alice, no, no, no". I am screaming hysterically now. Ben decides to join me and begins to wail too as I slip and slide trying to regain my feet. Then I hear it, someone shouting, getting louder as they approach us.

"Mummy, mummy, my daughter's shout is music to my ears, I spin round only to see Alice, minus her hat, coming toward me, hand in hand with her daddy. My husband's face is a picture of both confusion and amusement, he is trying to contain the grin that is creeping across his face.

"Mummy, why are you on the floor?" Alice is now beside me, "oh look mummy, there is my hat, thought I had lost it, but you found it mummy, you are clever" Her words tumble out of her mouth as fast as the stream beside us. "See mummy, I found daddy, he was at the bus stop". My precious girl is now right beside me, I put Ben down and wrap my arms around her tightly. The absurdity of the situation causing laughter to rise up, relief overflowing.

"Mummy you are all wet, you are funny mummy, shall we go home now?"

I nuzzle my face in her damp curls, "yes darling, let's go home".

The Secret

It was a typical Monday morning in the Doyle home. Nuala could hear her mum and dad downstairs. Occasionally shouting out, hoping to stir her two brothers and herself into getting up and dressed for school. Only if it wasn't a typical Monday she thought, Nuala remembered as her eyes peaked from under her warm safe duvet, she remembered the bomb that had gone off close to by to where she lived on the Falls Rd estate just the day before. She knew there would be repercussions to the loyalist community by the IRA, it was normal life for them. Living in this war zone was getting harder and harder she thought as she raised herself from her comfortable bed, ready to face the day. Her mind was racing, would Stephen be ok?

What if the next bomb was close to his home, she didn't want to think about such horrors, but the thoughts wouldn't leave her mind that morning. Downstairs the topic of conversation from her parents was all about the previous day's events, reminding Nuala and her brothers to be careful. As usual her dad was dropping her younger brothers

Aiden and Declan at primary school on his way to work as an electrician, Nuala's mum walked part way with her daughter to the bus stop where she headed to work in town at the hair salon, leaving Nuala to make her own way to school alone. The was a lingering smell of burning and the air was thick and smoke, a smell she knew only too well, living amid the troubles.

As she hurriedly walked the rest of way to school, she couldn't wait for her first glance of Stephen, who would be waiting across in his usual spot. A fleeting moment to see each other before they went to their different schools for the day, looking forward to seeing him later. There he was she turned the corner, his backpack over his shoulder, his blonde hair immaculately styled as always and his navy blue uniform pristine. Nuala's face lit up as he saw him, his beaming smile said everything she needed to know, his ice blue eyes glistening as she walked up the road on the opposite side. How she wished she could just run over the road to him, but she knew the dangers were all too real and the consequences for them both if they were seen, so those precious few moments we're all they could share till later. Despite the road being busy with other pupils heading to either Methodist College where Stephen was a pupil and St Mary's Catholic girls' school where Nuala studied, neither noticed anyone, or anything else around for that brief time. It was like they were on another plane, in a parallel universe, despite trying to linger and stay in the moment, it was over all too soon as Nuala reached her school gates. She smiled and turned back Stephen was still watching her and Nuala's tummy did a flip as she turned and made her way into school.

Stephen's morning had started much as usual his younger brother waking him up from the bedroom they shared.

"Come on, mammy says, up" his brother Andrew shouted

Stephen wasn't much of a morning person but knowing he'd see Nuala before his days started at school got him from his bed easier. Finally, Stephen got his turn in the bathroom once his older sister Megan have finished getting ready for college, he made sure his hair was right before heading down to the family. In much the same way as in Nuala's family, talk was of the bomb and the fear of more violence that would come in retaliation. Stephens parents we're rushing as they had to leave for their jobs and Stephens dad always dropped his mum off at the offices where she was a cleaner before heading to the shop where he worked as a butcher on the Shankill Rd. Stephen sister left shortly after for college when her friends knocked as usual, leaving Stephen and his brother Andrew to make sure the house was locked up and secure before leaving to walk to school. Andrew always caught up with his friends from his class in the lower year, which suited Stephen as it meant he could wait to see Nuala without any interruption. He arrived at the usual spot waiting eagerly to catch a glimpse of the girl who had stolen his heart. Each second seemed like an hour as he stood there impatiently until from around the corner finally, he saw her, her long ginger hair looked beautiful as she walked along the road. Her school bag on her shoulder, maroon uniform looking as perfect as she was, he thought. Nuala's smile was almost coy, so not to attract too much attention, her beautiful deep green eyes where amazing he thought as he said to himself "that's my girl" with a sense of pride not being able to take his eyes from hers, but that moment was all too quickly over.

Throughout the day the secret couple used to stay connected on their mobile phones, of course they went under a pseudonym name, they knew they had to be incredibly careful and vigilant in case they were caught, texting each other at lunch time and after school when they could arrange to meet. Life was so difficult for these two young loves, ordinarily if they lived anywhere else, they knew their lives and relationship would be so different and accepted, sadly not in the north of

Ireland. Religion was so powerful, and the community divisions cut deep, so deep that they knew they would never be accepted from either side of the divide, no mixing, it was simple those were the rules.

The wall that divided the city's communities was enforcing this belief. Each side of the wall was self-sufficient within its confines, with them having their own shops, schools, businesses, pubs other forms of recreation and facilities. No mixing was tolerated but, in fact it was despised and just not accepted, but the people upheld these beliefs and feelings, consequently instilling them in the younger generations. Making sure there was no need for people living on either side of the divide to interact, it was hatred.

That was apart from Nuala and Stephen, two young people who didn't feel or understand what they were doing was wrong, they weren't hurting anyone. They met completely by accident 12 months previous on a scorching summer day, which was unusual in Belfast, Nuala had been walking in Cave Hill Country Park. Her best friend Orla was away on holiday with her family leaving Nuala with quite a lot of spare time in the summer holidays, her classes at Irish dancing had also taken a breakthrough the summer months. It was while since she had been out walking, so feeling at a loose end with her parents at work and her younger brothers at their grandmas, she decided to go for a walk to fill her day. As the sun was beating down with not a cloud in the sky, she decided to stop and take a break on a nearby bench and take in the beautiful views around her. She spent a few minutes sat daydreaming while wondering what her friend Orla was doing in Spain. Nuala was startled by someone asking if she minded that they sit down and shared the bench

"Not at all" ... she replied, looking at this young lad who roughly looks around her age. She couldn't help but notice that he had the most piercing blue eyes. They soon started to chat and introduced themselves to each other, quickly establishing that they were the same age, however, realising very soon that Nuala was Catholic and Stephen Protestant when they asked each other where they went to school. They both felt nervous talking, as this was against what they had been brought to do. knowing that they shouldn't even be talking to each other really didn't seem to matter they were just two young people innocently talking ... who where they hurting?

They laughed and soon discovered they had so much in common, music, the same bands, even football apart from supporting different teams, they talked and talked. Nuala began to relax in Stephens company, she shared with him her

hobby of Irish dancing and Stephen shared that he played football for his school. They seemed to talk for what seemed like hours with neither wanted the day to end, but knowing she had to get home Nuala explained that her parents would notice she was late and might start asking questions.
Stephen and Nuala knew they could only safely walk so far together without risking being seen by somebody each knew. Stephen said to Nuala that he would love to see her again but as much as Nuala wanted to, she was hesitant, as she was aware that there would be no end of the trouble for each of them if they were found out, the thought of having to lie to her parents wasn't exactly something that was comfortable for her. Stephen seeing, she had been thrown into deep thoughts by his question told Nuala it was ok if she felt it was too dangerous and would respect her decision. Nuala's head was whirling with thoughts of knowing this was such a bad idea, yet her tummy was summersaulting at the thought of seeing Stephen again despite the dangers. "Don't worry yourself Nuala "Stephen said, as they got close to where they would have to part company safely, when Nuala turned and asked Stephen if he would like her number. Stephen's smile said it all and quickly grabbed his mobile from his pocket..." Ready" Stephen said as Nuala gave him her number, but telling him, begging him only to txt and never call her in case it wasn't safe. Knowing

the dangers for them both Stephen agreed and asked Nuala to do the same in return. That is how this young love had started, with determination, excitement, and hope.

Over the months they met in secret arranging meetings over their mobile phones each telling the families they were at friends' homes or out with friends and only trusting a friend each with the most dangerous of secrets. Orla, Nuala's best friend was entrusted with her secret, yet voicing her concerns about safety and repercussions if she was caught, hoping to talk her friend out of this madness, but she could tell from Nuala's face it was pointless as she was determined. Wayne, Stephen's best friend knowing how dangerous it was for his friend also tried to get Stephen to change his mind but knowing he had never seen his friend so eager to be with this girl, whatever he said he knew he couldn't dissuade him from continuing. Both of their trusted friends unhappy, frightened, and very worried if the worst was to happen for them. The couple found places to meet in secret always making sure to arrive and leave separately so not to be seen, they deeply wanted to be able to walk along the street together and for Stephen to walk Nuala home, but they knew this was just a pipe dream. So, stealing time away from their homes, where they were less likely to be seen or recognised was the price for being together, but always looking over their shoulder.

As their relationship deepened, they talked for hours about a future once school and college was over, Stephen wanted to become a motor mechanic and Nuala had always wanted to go into medicine, they both hoped and prayed that life in their home city would and could change, and a lasting peace would eventually become real and allow a new life to start. For now, things were as they had always known, bombs going off on both sides of the divide on a regular basis, sporadic shootings on the streets and soldiers everywhere. It felt like a world away to Nuala and Stephen and as sad and terrible as this situation was, they continued to live in a war zone. Yes, both knew families and knew people who had lost loved ones, it wasn't a situation they had wanted to live in. They were born into it and never given the choice, their young lives were dictated by others, by religion and by history, but they believed they were strong enough to eventually live a life together free from conflict, from violence, from the troubles.

As their relationship continued, after leaving school each getting the grades to attend colleges for their chosen career paths both Stephen and Nuala felt a step closer to being together. Nuala had to make university choices, easy, she thought to herself. Stephen was doing well in college and was predicted to pass with flying colours which pleased him, Nuala on the other hand had to apply to universities to continue her studies, the conversation with her parents had started well, they expected her to study in Belfast, however on telling them her plan was to go to England they were dumbfounded. Nuala reeled off her planned speech telling them she had researched and felt better opportunities for her were in Manchester, she showed her parents online to strengthen her argument, but saddened as she wasn't being completely honest with them. They took some time, Nuala's parents agreeing if that is where she wanted to study, they would support her. Application submitted she just had to get the grades needed now, Nuala knew it was the right decision to move to Manchester, despite her parents' reservations for both her reasons, her future career, and her relationship. Planning together Stephen and Nuala started looking at flats to rent online, looking for Stephen a job, all appeared more fruitful for them and the future together despite neither ever living away from home not to mention across the water, it seemed the answer.

 A couple of months went by when Nuala received an offer to study medicine at Manchester University after having an interview, all subject of course to her A level results, she was ecstatic, she knew this was it, the answer to all their prayers and she couldn't wait to tell Stephen. Nuala decided to wait to tell him her news until she next saw him literally in the next few days, she wanted to see the reaction on his face when she told him. That weekend the couple were meeting on Sunday as he worked in the butcher's Saturdays and it was late when he would finish after cleaning the shop etc, Nuala spent Saturday with Orla, excited to share her news with her trusted friend, they had arranged to have a girly day out shopping in the city. Orla had always been Nuala's confident and was so happy for both her best friend and Stephen when she heard the news, knowing after all these secret years it was ending and they could start their lives properly together. The girls enjoyed a lovely day together despite the terrible weather on that Saturday, Nuala had text from Stephen as usual on his breaks at the shop, the girls had lunch, all was well apart from them getting soaked in the rain. Waiting for the bus the girls continued chatting and laughing when an all too familiar loud noise could be heard in the distance, they knew it wasn't too close but still knowing what it was, brought an eerie silence around them. Both girls automatically reached for the phones to let their families no they were both OK, it was the normal routine sadly, Nuala of course texting Stephen as well. As the girls boarded the bus to leave the city each was wondering where the explosion they had heard happened. They continued to chat through the journey, Nuala checked her phone a couple of times to see if Stephen had replied, there was a message from her mum but no other, he's busy she thought. Nearing the girls stop, an elderly couple had got on the bus, the girls over heard them talking discussing the explosion and explaining where it had taken place, Nuala's face drained in colour, getting off the bus Orla kept an arm on Nuala to steady her, Orla suggested they both went back to her house so they could try to find out more information, continually looking at her phone Nuala agreed, there was no text from Stephen.

Once back at Orla's she had to tell her friend that the reports were saying the explosion was in the area of Stephen's shop, Nuala felt sick not having heard from Stephen, her mind was racing with different scenarios playing out in her head as the tears she had tried to hold started to fall. Orla tried to comfort her telling her Stephen was probably helping injured people or he'd lost his phone in the commotion, eventually Nuala's phone lit up, a text. Grabbing for it, it was Wayne, Stephen's friend the text read....

"The bomb had gone off outside the butcher's shop and it had taken full impact. No news on the injured yet, I'll text later when I know more"

Nuala was numb, she just sat rocking in Orla's bedroom, her whole body felt frozen with fear. The silence in Orla's bedroom was deafening as the girls sat waiting for news, Nuala's phone lit up again. Wayne again ...

I'm afraid its bad news, Stephen was involved. He's dead!

The phone slipped from her shaking hand.

Nuala's life was shattered "Not Stephen" she cried unable to be consoled by Orla.

Nuala attended her beloved Stephens funeral but from a distance, the tears still flowing. Nuala had to pretend at home everything was fine, it was anything but fine, the pretence continued, Nuala had decided to follow her and Stephen's dream she believed she had to for them both.

In the September Nuala left Belfast for Manchester and her room in halls and the start of a new life. Her parents went with her to help her move in, Nuala was terrified she had made a mistake, but knowing deep down it was right, Belfast had taken Stephen from her she was determined to follow the dream they had planned together, she knew he was with her she could feel his presence. It had been a long day, up early for the ferry after saying goodbye to her brothers and of course Orla, once in her room bed made, books and laptop all set up, clothes put away, Nuala's mum thought she'd leave the rest for her daughter to finish herself. They all went for a lovely meal together before Nuala's parents had to leave to get the ferry home. Many cuddles and kisses later after waving her parents off, Nuala took a deep breath and made her way back to her room. Opening the door, she reached into her bag and pulled out her prized possession ... a photo of herself and Stephen. Kissing the frame and placing it on her bedside table, as she closed her room door saying quietly to herself.... "Let's do this" ....

End of Term Final Feast

LUCY

OK, so, big breaths, time to check everything. I'll count my pastry cases one more time, just to check I have enough ready for all of the guests – plus a dozen or more spare in case of breakages. They've been pre-baked, blind, earlier today – lots of cutting out of grease-proof paper rounds for them – and I had to borrow dried beans and rice from a couple of my mates as I didn't have enough of my fancy porcelain baking beans to go round. They were a present from Daniel, for our anniversary of getting together! That's why I like them the best. (The dried pulses do work too though.) I'll look out to see if I can return the favour – they may well need help getting the mains and desserts out later. Paddy's on desserts and Vanessa and Harry are working together on the mains. I hope I've chosen a good size for my cases. They're fairly little ones as I'm on the first starter – but I don't want them too small, or they could look mean. I think I've got them about right. Bijou, you might say. And with the filling I've chosen, they look really pretty made up! Asparagus, beetroot, red pepper, and goat's cheese filling. Hope I won't be marked down for having too many ingredients – it's just a few small pieces of red pepper but they really add to the colour. Just hope all of them have that crisp bite to the pastry, like the one I sampled this morning after my quick dummy run . . .

DANIEL

Oh, the relief! I've practised this consommé so many times this term, since I got a good mark with that first one, we did in class, but you never know how it's going to turn out on the day! First, you have to cook up a stupendous broth, full of intense flavour, otherwise there's not a lot of point, is there. I've used beef mince, carrots, leek, and thyme. But then, the magic of the dish is in the presentation of a clear consommé, and that involves removing all the bits and pieces that put the flavour in there in the first place, by adding enough whisked egg whites, first to a little of the stock separately, and cooking it in, to create that raft which will catch any solid components . . . don't worry! Nothing will be wasted. "Always remember", shouts our tutor, Mattie, "Nose to tail, we always use nose to tail in these kitchens – and that applies to vegetarian dishes too!"

There's Lucy across the far side of the kitchen, counting her cases. She's the best thing that's ever happened to me. Apart from getting into cooking of course. OK, maybe even more than that. I think she feels the same way about me. Oh, I do so hope I'm right. We can make a good life together.

Ooop – that's been simmering up now for over an hour now. It'll soon be time to strain it. I'd better get my fine sieves ready and line them with muslin cloth into clean saucepans.

Not to forget that we have several vegetarian guests tonight, who will be served portions of the tomato and basil-flavoured consommé I already prepared, first thing this morning. I just need to reheat it at the right time, and make sure the server has the specific list of guests – Mattie explained that he would be instructing the servers so I'm sure he'll have that well in hand.

After all, Mattie has more experience than the rest of us put together! He's worked in some fantastic, Michelin-starred restaurants. It's only his family commitments that has drawn him into tutoring back home. Too many late nights can break up a marriage. He's got his priorities right there, I think, now that he has children, especially as his youngest has special needs. Anyway – back too it!

Most of our guests will be served from jugs but I've a fancy idea for the high table where our tutors and VIPs will be seated. I'll need to warm those containers carefully, to the same temperature as the consommé, so that they won't steam up when I add it. That would spoil the magic just a bit.

LUCY

Time already? It always comes faster than you think – or want! But my filled tartlets are out of the oven, I have the small plates lined up with a few dressed rocket leaves on each, and we're transferring the tartlets, one onto each. (I say we – Paddy has his ice-cream churning and everything else ready for dessert so he's kindly alternating with me: more efficient that way, and I'll do the same for him.)

"Service please!"

Other college students are being paid for work experience and are lining up very nicely to take the small plates out to the guests.

My starter is all veggie so there is no complication over who gets what – except for . . . ah, here's Susie:

"I'm supposed to take a special one to a VIP with Coeliac" –

"Yes, right-o, here's the gluten-free tartlet on the plate with a gilded edge. You know which one she is?"

"Yes, Mattie Reynolds introduced me to her in person, to avoid risk of confusion. The special plate's a nice touch, too!"

"Can't be too careful, eh?" I added, with a nervous giggle. I was already a bag of nerves at the momentousness of the occasion, and now, doubly nervous at the idea of making someone unwell if we'd not got ourselves well enough organised.

With a final chuckle, Susie was gone, her laughter lost in the general noise of the crowd in the hall.

Paddy and I continued with our service, in silence, until the last plates had been taken to the guests. Only a few remained – already counted and known to be spares. We could all taste them later.

Phew. A huge sigh, my main work of the night completed and, apparently, successfully. I allowed myself a few moments to walk to the entrance to the hall.

They were eating my food. Judging from the way the plates were steadily being cleared, they were also enjoying my food. I was content. Really happy. I sighed again, pleased as well as, understandably, fatigued.

DANIEL

Lucy looks happy. Great.

Still, no time to think about that just now. I have the pre-heated jugs all ready, with the two types of consommés, also re-heated, and Mattie has pointed out which server is on the veggie Tomato and Basil option and has the lists of tables and names to match.

Also, I have preheated the crystal decanter. I happen to own one as it was left to me by my grandfather – the man who first taught me how to make bread by hand. I wouldn't be able to afford such an item otherwise! Lucy and I don't have much money, and we are already saving up, as we have plans to own a restaurant together one day.

Back to the present. It was a bit tricky to work out how to do this effectively, but I've done it a few times this term and I hope it's going to work tonight. By warming the decanter with hot water in advance, when I add the consommé, the glass remains clear and doesn't steam up.

OK, it's my turn to perform in public, instead of just behind the scenes.

Usually, the VIPs are served first, but they've not been served yet. Instead, I'm going to serve them myself. Using a dark green velvet cloth against the heat, I lift the decanter and carry it into the hall.

There is general chatter and clatter but, as people notice me, this quietens down. I see that Mattie has drawn Lucy to the hall entrance, as I asked him to.

After climbing the few steps to the stage, I turn and stand still for a moment, slowly raising the decanter just a little higher than my eye-line – and yes! George, in the lighting gallery, lights the spotlight onto my decanter of amber deliciousness, clear as you could want! Ah! It's worked!

There is a general intake of breath in the hall – and on the stage – and then applause breaks out and increases.

Let's not milk it!

I break the pose and, with a smile, serve each VIP guest and tutor from my decanter, chatting nonchalantly with them, asking how they are enjoying the meal . . . and then slip out, in a modest fashion, but, secretly, dead chuffed at having brought off that nice bit of theatre!

LUCY & MATTIE

"Come with me, Lucy, just for a moment."

"I can't really, Mattie, because Harry and Vanessa are going to be getting the mains ready soon and may need some . . . Ok then!"

As Mattie is already leading me out of the kitchen, I can't really do anything but comply. Soon, we are standing just inside the hall, looking towards the stage, hearing the hush develop, then the gasp as Daniel stands there, holding the decanter up into the beam of the spotlight. The consommé is the colour of deep, precious amber, and it sparkles in the spotlight!

I have never seen Daniel do anything so dramatic. I am astonished – and impressed. He then quickly breaks his pose and, after that, behaves in a far more conventional manner, as he serves the beautiful beef consommé to our tutors and the VIP guests.

Just then, I hear Vanessa calling out to Harry. I glance at Mattie, who nods, and I go off to see what they wanted me to do.

THE AFTERMATH

Mattie, our tutor, was full of congratulations, with praise and complements for each and every one of us.

We'd already gone into the hall at the end of the dessert course, received a vote of thanks from the Chief VIP and notes of positive feedback from Mattie as the coordinator for the whole thing, and taken our bows to the sound of enthusiastic applause, but this was our informal gathering, chilling together over a glass of wine.

Suddenly, Mattie posed a specific question at Daniel.

"Daniel – what gave you the crazy idea to serve hot beef consommé in a whisky decanter? And to get a spotlight shining on it? It was a magical effect – a delight – and, I have to tell you, I've never seen the like of it before!"

Looking startled, Daniel hesitated. Then, slowly, and stuttering just a bit, he explained, "Well, Mattie, I can't afford a ring."

The room fell silent.

"I mean, well, I could. I could spend out a bit of money on something second-rate – but, no, I can't afford the kind of ring I would like to buy for Lucy. So, that was my idea. My inspiration if you like. To create something that might just do, for now, in place of spending money that we are trying to save up! We want to own a restaurant one day."

Lucy was staring, in a state of confusion, a bit shocked, wondering whether to be happy but, just a bit mystified.

Daniel almost shouted, "Lucy – my inspiration was an engagement ring – one I can't readily afford right now – but the lovely clear glow of a well-made consommé put me in mind of . . ."

Lucy interrupted: "Yes! Daniel, yes, I will marry you. Rings can wait!"

The room erupted in cheering and laughter, and everyone rushed in to give their friends big hugs to celebrate them, and what they had found to share with each other.

Meet the Writers

Denise Fedigan

A native Wiganer, Denise, is the facilitator of the "Away with Words" writing for pleasure group. She is a serial hobbyist, writing being one of them. Her blog Milly is Metres from Madness kept her going throughout the pandemic.

Denise writes everything from speeches and poetry to letters and stories simply to keep herself entertained. It is her pleasure to direct the traffic in the group and keep everything moving along.

In This Book

George of the Grange – Saved from God's waiting room, can George find romance in the last chapter of his life …

Diggle Junction – Can Larry find the strength to face his Nemesis and return to life again…

On Amazon

The Eaglesfield Visitor – The Adventures of Brendan and his friends in the lake district National Park – An illustrated story of friendship and lessons in life for children around the world. Age 4-9

Still Living a Great Life – A memoir of her journey through life and the obstacles along the way.

Wendy Bate

Born and bred in Cheshire, Wendy is now retired after completing forty years in the NHS. Happily married with two daughters, and four grandchildren, Wendy is an avid reader and has a particular interest in historical fiction. She also enjoys all forms of handicrafts, including sewing, knitting, embroidery, and toy making to name but a few. She is currently writing her first novel.

Rescued - *A heart rending tale about an ill-treated dog who finds her forever home. A story of how love and trust can overcome anything.*

Coming Home - *A true ghost story about an old man who, after his death, returns to his family home only to find he no longer owns it.*

Frederick Peverill - *Following the death of her parents, Madeleine not only inherits the family home, but a very special cat into the bargain. Little does she know it can talk.*

Debra Ball

Debra is a retired nurse from Wigan in the Northwest of England. She has read books all her life and especially loves memoirs. Reading has been a passion since childhood. She loves to travel and has worked abroad. She is interested in adventure and people who live unusual lives.

Be Careful What You Wish For *...An adventurous traveller finds the grass isn't always greener.*

Julie Scollon

Julie, a born-again Christian, is a retired NHS secretary who was raised in Manchester but has called Wigan, Lancashire her home for the last 40+ years. She loves to craft having tried many over the years, now just concentrating on writing, knitting/crochet, and drawing /painting. When not crafting she loves spending time with her family including her husband and her four adorable young grandchildren.

Julie is currently in the process of writing her first book, a non-fiction book about Christianity.

The Dance ... *A tale of love and romance in war torn England.... with a twist*

Belle ... *Family can be your worst enemy .... a tale of betrayal and deceit*

The Yellow Raincoat ... *Determination and defiance in one so young*

Maggi Dilworth

Mandi is a northern lass who was born and brought up in St Helens for the early part of her life before moving to Wigan. Happily married to David, they have a blended family of three beautiful adult daughters along with their two cats Tallulah and Geordie. Words have always proved to be very powerful to Mandi in various forms from quotes, poems, phrases and of course books, this is what brought Mandi to writing.

A serial hobbyist starting with a love of card making and papercraft she's happy to try anything new, she enjoys sewing, knitting, photography, wildlife, supporting her team Liverpool FC and of course reading, she is in the process of writing her first book. Mandi has a love of all wildlife and animals, but seals are her passion, she enjoys photographing them in their natural habitat, this has taken her all over the UK (so far). Mandi is also an active fundraiser for a local cat charity, so likes to keep herself busy learning, trying and by doing.

Spreading my Wings @ My Comfy Nest

Sometimes you have to move out of your comfort zone and challenge your fears, sometimes with the help of a friend.

Anne Clayton

Anne and her husband live in the Northwest of England and have just celebrated their forty years ruby wedding. They have two beautiful grown-up daughters and two amazing grandsons. After surviving working as a front-line worker during the covid pandemic, she has recently retired after forty-one exciting years in the NHS as a nurse and midwife. She is a social creature and joined the creative writing group," A Way with Words." To meet new friends and keep her brain active. Her goal is to write children's books. Anne's other hobbies include baking, gardening, swimming, travel and catching up with her family and friends.

The Last Goodbye ...Amelia has just left her parent's villa in Alicante. She was catching a routine flight home, as she had to work the next day, but events take an unexpected turn.

Festival Child ... It was on my bucket list to attend Glastonbury 2023. It was amazing and Elton's headline performance ensured it was historical event, but it surpassed even my wildest dreams when I found a baby.

Joanna Treasure

Joanna, often known as Jo, lives in Lancashire with her husband and three adult sons. During her demanding and stressful first career as a hospital pathologist, she found it cathartic to enjoy writing music and poetry, as a means of self-expression and light relief. She has only recently started to experiment with fiction.

A Day in the life of a Postie.... *Finding new love can be scary - how can you know for sure they're right for you?*

End of Term Final Feast ... *All the pressure of getting it on the table, combined with the inspiration to celebrate something truly special.*

Elizabeth Scally

Elizabeth Scally was born and bred in Wigan. A recently retired community nurse, married with two grown up daughters, she likes to travel with her husband and friends. Her fondness for reading starting in childhood and she has herself written many short stories for over thirty years, but until now, has never published.

A serial hobbyist, from an early age being a knitter for family and charities. recently she has tried new crafts for example quilling, card making and likes the challenge of new to her crafts She donates some of her spare time volunteering at a local community pantry which prevents foods going to land fill.

The Prom.... *It's become a new norm where we read about others good fortune wishing we had the same, or do they actually have what they say.*

The Old Tin Box.... *Where the past gets dug up.*

Alison Lamb

Now retired after many years working in the textile industry, Alison is finding new ways to fill her time. A busy grandmother who enjoys cooking, sewing, gardening, walking and a glass or two of red wine. Her greatest passion is Northern Soul music, enjoying listening and throwing a few shapes on the dance floor.

The Surprise *... Pauline returns to her home village to care for her ageing mother after years of living and working in the city. Her new job leads her to a startling discovery about her father's past.*

Mandi O'Neill-Hugill

Hi, I'm Mandi, I'm a northern lass born in St Helens but lived in Wigan most of my life. I'm happily married to David and our blended family consists of three adult girls and to fur babies Tallulah and Geordie. I have always loved to read I find words in quotes, poems, and books to be very powerful, which is what brought me to writing. I love to craft, knit, and sew I'm also passionate about wildlife especially seals and I travel to photograph them in their natural habitat, I also fundraise for a local cat charity so as you can tell I like to be busy with some project or other.

The Secret – *Can love overcome the divide in a war-torn community?*